Death
on the
Funeral Yacht

A 1950s San Francisco Mystery

Mary Miller Chiao

Death on the Funeral Yacht

ISBN: 978-0-578-70718-1

Published by Mary Miller Chiao, San Jose, California, 95129.

Printed in the United States of America.

Publisher's Note: This book is a work of fiction. Names, characters, places, and incidents are either the product of the author's imagination or are used fictitiously, and any resemblance to actual persons, living or dead, events, or locales is entirely coincidental.

Front cover image the Golden Gate Bridge. Original image from Carol M. Highsmith's America. Digitally enhanced by rawpixel. Public domain. Rawpixel.com ID: 2110387 CCO 1.0 Universal.

Title page image of the Cliff House 1951. Justmerriam, Mike Roberts Production. Commons.wikimedia.org/wiki/file:Cliff_House_Comp.jpg. Postcard in the public domain.

Luanna K. Leisure, Little White Feather Graphic Designer.

To order additional books go to: **http://www.LuLu.com, Amazon.com or Barnesandnoble.com.**

marymillerchiao@gmail.com
www.MaryMillerChiao.com

Special Acknowledgements

A grateful thank you to Annick Shinn, Ursula Meier, Rosemarie Niles, and Irene Groot who listened to this story every Thursday afternoon at Annick's house and encouraged me to continue.

Prologue

I am sure if Jay Lucas had known he would accompany Susannah's ashes into San Francisco Bay that Sunday afternoon in 1959, he would never have stepped onto the deck of the yacht.

"Socialite Heiress Takes Celebrity Attorney Lover with Her," screamed the headline in the *San Francisco Chronicle* the next morning.

The public's appetite for scandalous news seemed insatiable. Reporters from every major newspaper in the country descended on our *City by the Bay,* determined to dig up all the sordid details of the tragedy. They followed those of us who were passengers on board the yacht, blatantly intruding in our daily lives with endless questions about the gruesome death.

Readers flocked to newspaper stands, waiting for the latest edition. Radios and televisions were set to news channels. Shocked politicians and Hollywood celebrities were endlessly interviewed. The death of Jay Lucas was the lead feature in Walter Winchell's *New York Daily Mirror* column for months and the primary topic on his Sunday night radio program.

Everyone talked about that night. The media dubbed the death of Jay Lucas one of the great mysteries of the 1950s.

It had been clear and sunny in the early afternoon when we set sail with Susannah's ashes from the pier in San Francisco on *The Dearly Departed*. There were thirty of us, close friends and associates of Susannah and Jay. The gentle breeze and the salty smell of the sea lulled our senses as we watched the San Francisco waterfront recede in the distance and marveled at the breathtaking views of Angel Island and Alcatraz. Our yacht cruised past the picturesque towns of Sausalito and Tiburon, then sailed under the Golden Gate Bridge, turned, and ran with the wind back into the Bay.

In the late afternoon, with the sun descending into the horizon, we gathered on the deck for our final goodbyes. Jay Lucas stood at the stern of the yacht staring into the heavens. His bright Hawaiian shirt contrasted with the muted colors of the sky and the crimson bridge in the background. He turned his teary eyes briefly toward us, and I saw his lips tremble. Slowly, as if his arm was filled with lead, he raised it over the rail and let Susannah's ashes gently cascade from the container into the calm water.

A quiet pall settled over the group as the sun disappeared and twilight enveloped us. We stood there reverently, watching the fog roll in. No one wanted to move.

Suddenly, Lucas started shaking his fists and yelling at the heavens like a maniac. We were shocked at this unexpected change in his behavior. Some of the male passengers rushed to assist him, but he fought them like a mad man.

As if responding to the horror of the scene, the weather changed abruptly. The gentle breeze became cold and blustery. The skies darkened, and drizzling rain followed. Waves picked up and battered our yacht from side to side. We pushed and shoved each other in our haste to reach the safety of the boat's interior. I stumbled and fell to the deck. Struggling to rise, I saw Jay Lucas break free from the men dragging him to the cabin. He reached out to me. Just as the boat dipped toward the swelling waters, a strong gust of wind blew him sideways. His arms flailed helplessly. Unable to regain his balance, he fell backwards over the side of the yacht.

The captain yelled instructions to the crew while trying to keep the yacht steady in the turbulent waters. My wet clothes clung to my body, and my eyes stung from the salt mist. I wrestled my way against the wind to the side of the yacht and watched them direct lights on the struggling figure. They tossed life rings to him and tried to snag his clothing with long hooked poles.

The engine's motor droned on and on as it accelerated sharply, then slowed, then quickened again. My stomach lurched from the violent rolling. I held onto the gunwales, my hands like iron grips, and threw up the contents of my stomach into the churning water.

Waves continued to smash ruthlessly against the yacht. The captain yelled for lifejackets. Below me, Jay Lucas screamed and thrashed wildly in the dark maelstrom. I saw him swallowed by the waves, then reappear, only to vanish again.

It seemed an eternity before the captain called the authorities ship-to-shore. I huddled in my coat with the others while we waited for the police boats. My face felt wet from the mist, its salt combining with the taste of vomit in my mouth. I was cold and wet, bleeding from shards of glass that I had fallen into on the deck.

At last the police boats arrived. Their sirens blended with the wind, the splashing sounds of rough water, and the ghostly moans of the foghorn. Their eerie searchlights scanned the dark bay.

Our captain left them to their appalling task and turned the boat around toward the pier.

When we docked, patrol cars lined the wharf, their headlights illuminating the drizzle. Officers walked up the gangplank holding umbrellas that threatened to blow away. They escorted us off one by one.

Waiting reporters in their hooded trench coats seemed oblivious to the nasty weather. They followed at our heels like pesky little yapping dogs, shouting questions and blinding us with flashes from their cameras.

I remember being led to a Ford Custom 300, its red-domed beacon light spinning round and round. Someone opened the door, pushed the seat forward, and helped me into the back. I grabbed the blanket that lay on the seat and buried my head in it.

I am the last person alive who sailed on board *The Dearly Departed* that fateful day over sixty years ago. Through the decades, reporters have tried to interview me, but I remained silent.

I am old and sick. It is time to tell my story. Let me start at the beginning, and, forgive me in advance if I digress, but I have earned the right to speak about that day in my own way and at my own speed.

Chapter 1

It began in 1950. I had worked for pennies as a secretary/receptionist at an insurance company in San Francisco while attending school at night. It wasn't easy, but I did it, barely making enough money to support myself in a small studio apartment. After earning my bachelor's degree, I continued on to law school where, at the age of twenty-eight, I graduated with a Juris Doctor degree, one of two females in my class. I easily passed the bar exam.

Elated, I gave notice and started my search for employment as an attorney. Day after day, I mailed applications and walked the streets, submitting my resume to one law firm after another; but San Francisco was a bastion of male lawyer supremacy, and the few offers I got were piddling. I watched the male members of my graduating class find employment easily.

Finally, on the last day of November, after a miserable Thanksgiving, my phone rang. The office of Jay Lucas, one of the most prominent attorneys in San Francisco, was on the line.

I arrived for my interview at his prestigious Pacific

Street offices the next day, a damp and blustery Friday, December 1, 1950. I felt and looked cold and windblown. My wet bangs stuck to my forehead, and I had forgotten my comb. My cardigan sweater hid the pinched-waist dress that was too tight, and my feet hurt from the insufferable high heels that were fashionable. The receptionist, whose name plaque read "Maude Lind," raised her nose high and told me to sit while she announced my arrival on the intercom.

"Miss Jane Kitteridge is here."

She didn't wait for an answer but resumed typing a stack of envelopes, pausing several times to sniff the air as if something reeked. There was no one else in the area but me.

I sat down on the oversized couch and arranged the hem of my dress to cover my knees. On the table in front of me lay several magazines and a large brown leather album titled *Welcome to the Lucas Law Firm.* I opened it and flipped through pages of newspaper clippings about Jay Lucas and his successful practice. Several times while I read, the phone rang. The firm had a modern telephone system, and the receptionist simply pressed a few buttons to answer the call. In my previous position, I operated a manual switchboard. Long cords had to be inserted into and pulled from jacks on a high back panel to connect and disconnect calls.

Twenty minutes later, a deep voice growled from the intercom, "Show her in."

I rose, patted my tangled hair, smoothed down my dress, and followed the receptionist through double doors to a room reeking of Bay Rum aftershave and cigarettes. A beautiful red Persian rug with the tree of life design lay over a polished wood floor. Nineteenth century paintings of California scenery and photographs by Ansel Adams adorned one of the walls.

Jay Lucas rose from behind a large glass-covered mahogany desk and motioned for me to sit. I guessed him to be in his early forties. He was a tall, handsome man, his hair a distinguished salt-and-pepper color, cut in the style of the movie star, Tony Curtis. He wore a single-breasted sleek Italian suit molded to his body. Gold monogrammed cufflinks, a pocket square, and an antique tie clip completed his outfit. I glanced at his feet. They were encased in polished black pointed-toe shoes. He had my resume in his hand.

"In the last six months, I've received three of these," he said. "If I've gotten that many, so has every law firm in San Francisco. You don't give up easily." He lit a Chesterfield with his reptile skin-covered Ronson lighter, inhaled deeply, and let the smoke waft out in my face. "I called your law school and spoke with your professors. They told me you are exceptionally intelligent and one of their best students but will never go far because, not only are you boring and mousey, you have no looks whatsoever." He took another drag. "I don't mind having a 'boring and mousey' unattractive girl working for me, but not out front. Your office will be in a back room. My legal secretary has been terminated, and I need to fill the position immediately with someone familiar with the law and very good, which I have been assured by your professors and your former employer, you are."

"But I don't want to be a secretary, Mr. Lucas," I insisted. "I applied for a position in your firm as an attorney." My right foot, cramped in the shoe, had gone to sleep, and, I was afraid if I stood up, I would stumble out of his room.

He stared at me. "You should rethink your position and consider my offer to be somewhat like one of the law clerks that work for a chief justice. A woman cannot make it as an attorney in this town. I'm doing you a favor. You can tell your friends you work for Jay Lucas." He turned his back and reached for the decanter on his credenza. "Besides," he paused while removing the stopper and pouring the golden liquor into a snifter, "I know you need a job, and I will pay you well."

He was right. I was down to my last hundred dollars. I accepted his offer.

4

Chapter 2

I arrived at the Pacific Street offices of the Lucas Law Firm on Monday, December 4, 1950, and walked through spotless glass doors onto the plush wall-to-wall beige carpet in the reception area. A large framed photograph of Jay Lucas shaking hands with President Truman stared down at me. Next to it were pictures of JL smiling proudly with Governor Earl Warren and Mayor Elmer Robinson. Tufted leather chairs and a matching couch complemented the paneled walls. A rectangular glass table with ashtrays on each side stood in front of the couch. The February edition of *Life* lay on top of several magazines, a photograph of Gregory Peck from his latest movie, *Twelve O'clock High*, on the cover. The room was quiet, the atmosphere heavy. Various male colognes blended with the smell of coffee.

The receptionist's area was immaculate, her desk as shiny as the polished wood floor. She was bent over, watering a tall *ficus benjamina* with a copper can. The spreading canopy of the tree threatened to engulf her, a rather pleasant thought. She gripped a feather duster in her left hand and carried a bag of coffee filters under her arm.

"The men are in a meeting this morning," she said, concentrating on her task without looking at me. "Your room is down the hall between Mr. Lucas's office and our law library. I put a set of keys to the building on your desk. If you have questions, see me. I'm in charge of all the girls." She stopped watering and inspected a leaf. I had been dismissed.

The warm wood walls continued down the hall. Nameplates on the first two doors to the left indicated the rooms were occupied by Marvin Basil, Esq., and Cyrus A. Qualms, Esq. To the right was the room of another attorney, Prescott Van Nostrand, III. Next to it, a door marked "Typing Pool" opened suddenly. I heard the nonstop clicking of Smith Corona keys and glimpsed a dark room with desks close together. A small brunette with a pencil over her ear scurried past me and disappeared down the hall behind another door marked "Conference Room." Angry male voices rose and fell when it opened and closed.

In the next room, chairs surrounded a large, round wooden table. A napkin dispenser sat next to an ashtray filled with stubbed out cigarettes, some with lipstick stains around the filter. The morning *Chronicle* lay folded open to an article about the Chinese Communist invasion of Korea and our subsequent involvement in the war. Against the wall, an avocado-green refrigerator stood next to a matching freestanding stove. A percolator gurgled on one of the burners. The smell of coffee was inviting so I walked in and glanced around. Cups and saucers had been placed upside down on a tray beside the sink. A white Formica counter over wood cabinets stretched the length of one wall. Someone had tacked a typewritten sheet of paper headed "Girls' Kitchen Cleanup" on the brown corkboard bulletin board above. My name had been penciled in for Thursdays.

No nameplate hung on my office door. The room was small, slightly larger than a walk-in closet. The walls were bare and painted a headache white. Piles of paper were strewn over the floor as if picked up by a tornado and dumped. A calendar, Rolodex, scotch tape holder, and two-holed punch lay among the debris. It would appear that whoever had previously held my position vacated suddenly, and with malice.

Several files and a checkbook lay on the credenza. A note written with black ink on a yellow-lined legal-sized pad had instructions for me. The handwriting resembled a doctor's prescription. I struggled to read.

"In meetings all day
Clean up room
Type letters
Prepare documents

Type personal checks
Charge bottle of L'Air du Temps by Nina Ricci at La Rouge
   Perfumery.

EVERYTHING ON MY DESK 8 A.M. TOMORROW!"

It was signed with a flourished, "*JL.*"

I walked to the window and looked out. Nimbus clouds ringed the building across the street like the halo on a dark angel. Below, bundled-up pedestrians cradling umbrellas hurried down the street and crossed against the light at the corner, anxious to get somewhere before raindrops fell.

I turned around, determined not to give in to self-pity. I had to replenish my bank account before I could resume my search. This position would simply be temporary. Besides a good salary, the firm provided medical and dental benefits.

I gathered the papers from the floor and laid them on the credenza, along with the two-hole punch, calendar, tape, and stapler.

"You've arrived," announced a deep voice behind me. I jumped and swung around. A side door to Jay Lucas's office stood open in back of my desk. He looked and smelled like he had just stepped out of the pages of *Esquire Magazine.* "I'll be out all day."

He pointed at my desk. "I see you found your work list

for today. Tomorrow morning I'll be dictating a couple of weeks' worth of letters so bring at least two steno pads into my office." He paused. "I'll see just how good your shorthand is." With that, he turned around and shut the door.

I sat down at the Smith Corona electric typewriter. Opening the desk drawer, I pulled out letterhead, carbon paper, and a couple of sheets of onionskin for the copies. I perused his drafts. Not only did his handwriting look atrocious, but there were cross outs everywhere. Arrows pointed all over the page and behind to the back. When he said draft, he should have added that it was extremely rough. I concentrated on each paragraph until I knew the point he wanted to make; then I reworked his words until everything sounded professional. I typed the letters, making one typo. Exasperated at my error, I pulled the original, the copies, and the carbon paper out of the typewriter, erased the typo on all, realigned the papers, and returned them to the typewriter to complete the letter. After that, I opened his checkbook. Invoices were crammed inside. I prepared checks for his signature, noting that he had accounts at several elite men's and women's stores, bars, and restaurants. The balance on his Tiffany statement alone topped a thousand dollars.

The legal volumes on the shelves of the floor-to-ceiling

bookcases in the firm's law library were impressive. It didn't take me long to find the appropriate forms for the documents he requested, but preparing them took time. I decided to forego lunch. The door opened and closed several times, but I didn't look up. I intended to prove to Jay Lucas that I could do everything on his list.

I finished at 7 p.m., walked into his office, and placed my day's work in his inbox. Framed pictures sitting on the credenza showed him hobnobbing with celebrities and politicians. My eyes focused on a photograph of an attractive heavily made-up blond woman wearing pearls that extended into the bodice of her low-cut red dress. I guessed her to be his current wife. I had read in the society pages that he was on his third, or was it his fourth? A brown leather calendar lay open to the week, a large gold fountain pen on top. He had lunch appointments every day, his companions identified with initials.

Tired, and hungry, I left the building and walked in the rain to the perfume store at Union Square. The saleswoman looked me up and down and said, "It is too late for me to call Mr. Lucas to confirm who you are. Come back in the morning." My head had begun to ache, my feet hurt, and my stomach growled. I looked at her nametag. "Mr. Lucas will be very upset if this bottle is not on his desk first thing tomorrow morning, Miss Hicks, and I'm sure he'll call your employer to complain."

She sprayed tissue paper with a L'Air du Temps tester; then wrapped a bottle of the perfume and placed the package in a French tricolor shopping bag.

I caught the bus on Market Street and put ten cents in the coin collector. The few passengers were either hunched over reading newspapers under the dim lights or staring blindly out the window. I seated myself in the back and watched the rain fall in puddles. The bus smelled of perspiration, stale food, and the sprayed tissue paper in the colorful boutique bag. The floor was littered with paper. We stopped at every corner till we got to Cabrillo Street and 38th Avenue. I stepped down in front of my apartment building, trudged through the rain to the front, then over the dirty carpet and up four flights to my studio apartment.

Pearl greeted me at the door. Even though my head pounded, my legs felt heavy, and my back hurt, I managed to open a can of cat food and spooned it onto a dish with some kibble. There was just enough to last until payday. A can of Campbell's Soup and a peanut butter sandwich would suffice for me. After a hot shower, I crawled into bed. The cat was already there.

Chapter 3

Over the next few months, I became acquainted with Jay Lucas and his law firm. JL, as he liked to be called, had made a name for himself by successfully representing several high profile clients in well-publicized lawsuits. You may remember that he handled the divorce of the French bombshell, Monique Francoeur, a B movie star. The charms of the voluptuous actress were hidden away when she arrived each day in court dressed in the uniform of a prim French schoolgirl. He combated assertions that she had committed adultery against her aged husband, the chairman of the board of one of the most profitable industrial corporations, by portraying her as an innocent girl who had been taken advantage of by a dirty old man. Need I mention that JL was sleeping with Monique during the entire trial?

Another headlined case you may remember was his defense of major league baseball centerfielder Nick Harwood, known for his fiery temper. Nick had jumped into the stands and slammed his glove into the face of a heckling fan. Unfortunately for Nick, the man's friend, a professional boxer, sunk his fist into Nick's crotch protector and bent it, along with its contents. The fan sued Nick, and he sued both the fan and the boxer.

JL successfully handled both cases, relishing the publicity and preening in the limelight.

Lucas fawned over people he thought were important. He would also call reporters and give them his opinion on newsworthy topics, ensuring his name would appear often in print.

Clients lined up at the law firm door, eager to tell their friends that Jay Lucas handled their legal needs.

With his flamboyant style and movie-star looks, he became the darling of San Francisco society. His goings-on were reported in the business and society columns where he was once referred to as "San Francisco's well-dressed answer to Perry Mason."

Not long after I started working for him, I noticed the picture of his wife smashed and sitting in his wastebasket. The next morning, he instructed me to pull out the prenuptial agreement from his files and prepare the divorce papers.

Pictures of JL with attractive, wealthy women appeared frequently in the newspaper. One pundit snidely remarked he couldn't decide who was more fashionably dressed, JL or his date. Lucas dined daily with beautiful companions at top restaurants like DiMaggio's, The Cliff House, and The Mark Hopkins. He had an uncanny ability to know when celebrities were in town and contacted their press agents with invitations to join him for lunch or dinner, making sure to alert the society page's photographers if a meeting had been arranged. A wine aficionado, he often hosted large parties at Napa Valley vineyards for which invitations were very much sought after.

JL owned an apartment building on Nob Hill and had converted the entire top floor to a luxury penthouse where he lived. He drove a black Jaguar XK120 two-seat roadster that could travel as high as 120 miles per hour. Maude told me he purchased it directly from England for $4,000 after he read "My Favorite Sports Car" by Clark Gable in the March 1950 issue of *Road & Track Magazine*. He paid for three parking spots in the small lot across from our building, and the royal carriage sat in the middle. I couldn't imagine driving a stick shift in San Francisco with our high hills, but that didn't bother him.

Although JL knew a lot of people, he didn't have any close friends. There were three guys he hung out with. I nicknamed them Huey, Dewey, and Louie because they were always together and acted like children. They had been students together at San Francisco State. All three held important well-paying jobs in the City. JL was the Alpha male in this small wolf pack. The men liked to be seen with him and hung on his every word. I found them rather creepy. Sometimes they would whisper in JL's office, and I heard those annoying male guffaws that follow dirty jokes.

They liked to attend the San Francisco 49ers football games at Kezar Stadium. The four of them sat close to the field and wore tan fishermen bucket hats with adjustable neck straps for protection from the low flying seagulls that flocked in for discarded food. After the games, they hung out at the local pub, celebrating victory or lamenting the 49ers loss. The group also favored the San Francisco State Dons basketball team.

Every couple of months, they would fly to Las Vegas for a weekend at the Fabulous Flamingo. They would spend their days swimming and gorging on the food, and their nights watching fabulous entertainment like the Dean Martin and Jerry Lewis show. One time when JL returned, he put all his receipts from the trip on my desk to file. Stuck inside was a paper listing phone numbers for Candy, Mocha, Starlene, Kitty, and Bambi. The first four had five stars after their names, but poor Bambi only had one. The four always returned tanned and tired from Vegas, their peckers probably wilted.

But, let me make it clear, Jay Lucas was extremely intelligent and very clever. He had worked hard to build up his law firm, and he had an excellent business reputation. The attorneys he hired were the best. They gathered first thing every Monday morning for a meeting. Each reported the status of his cases, and JL delegated responsibilities. He had no hesitation firing any of his lawyers, especially if they lost important cases, or clients.

Although JL stood out wearing the latest men's fashions, he ensured his attorneys did not outshine him. They wore the standard gray, black, or blue flannel single-breasted three-button jackets with narrow lapels and tapered trousers.

When new clients walked through the doors to our firm, JL assured them they would be taken care of royally, and they were. He kept those cases he felt would give him the most exposure and passed the rest off to his other attorneys.

Once Lucas told me he intended to write a book about himself. That did not surprise me. He was an arrogant and conceited man, given to namedropping. He instructed me to peruse the newspaper daily and cut out any item that mentioned his name, then paste the clipping into either of two large albums, one business, and the other social. I put the professional scrapbook on the reception table for clients to look at, and JL kept his personal scrapbook on his credenza, where he perused it frequently. He intended to use these records for reference when he sat down in his later years to write his autobiography.

There were days when JL was moody and angry. It was as if something inside of him clicked, and he became a different person. He could loudly praise someone, then turn around the next minute and complain about his or her incompetence. When JL was in one of these moods, a pall enveloped the entire law firm.

After a childhood of being shuffled from one foster family to the next, I knew how to blend into the woodwork when necessary. There were ways for me to avoid JL on his bad days and still do his work. His disparaging remarks about my looks and my clothes did not rile me since I had no plans to stay a long time with the firm.

After observing him those first few months, I came to believe that he had an uncanny ability to size people up. He identified their strengths and immediately seized on their weaknesses, filing the information in his head to be brought out when useful. I suspected that inside or outside of the courtroom, he was not the kind of person you wanted to upset.

My workload was heavy, and I frequently stayed late at the office. I gained hands-on experience in legal research and also learned the ins and outs of the San Francisco court system.

Several times Lucas grudgingly conceded he could find nothing wrong with my performance. JL liked my work, and why wouldn't he? He had hired a lawyer, a paralegal, and a secretary in one person.

After a few months, he started to assign me work that he would normally ask one of his assistant attorneys to research and prepare. It wasn't long before his clients were calling me directly with questions. That gave me hope that Lucas would consider the possibility of transitioning me from his secretary to one of his lawyers in the firm.

I was pleasantly surprised to find that Marla and I lived just a few blocks from each other on Cabrillo. We rode the same bus to work but got on at different stops. She was the brunette who rushed down the hall to the conference room in front of me on my first day of work. She took her job seriously, and I could tell she tried hard to please the men she typed for. Marla had been at the firm for three years and was happy with her job. The attorneys were nice to her and she liked the four other girls in the typing pool. She said JL was so difficult to work for he had gone through at least five secretaries since she started at the firm.

Marla's parents owned an Italian delicatessen on

Cabrillo. Her brother had been an early casualty of the Korean War that started in June 1950. He had enlisted in the army at the age of 18 and fought in World War II; then decided to stay with the military and was sent to Korea. He had been shot by a sniper and sent for recuperation to Letterman Army Hospital in the Presidio. The doctors said he would never walk again. I didn't know much about the Korean War. It seemed like we had just ended World War II and here we were fighting again.

Because I usually worked late, I didn't ride home with Marla, but in the mornings she would save me a seat. She was quiet and shy and knew everything about everyone in the firm. I enjoyed hearing the gossip. She suggested JL should have had his own soap opera series because the office was always abuzz with gossip about his latest marriage or stormy romance. Soon we started to hang out, sometimes to shop or see a movie. Because we both lived close to the ocean, on good days we would take our sun hats and towels and lie on the sand, smothering our bodies in baby oil while gabbing and listening to the surf. Sometimes we'd walk along the beach up to the Cliff House. Golden Gate Park was close so there were days spent at the museum, the aquarium, or the Japanese Tea House. Fleishacker Zoo was another destination. At work, if we were both free at lunchtime, we'd eat in Chinatown or Fisherman's

Wharf. On occasion, we walked to North Beach, grabbed sandwiches from a deli, and ate on the benches of the park in front of Saints Peter and Paul Church on Filbert.

Chapter 4

My first year at the Lucas Law Firm flew by. Except for the time I spent with Marla on weekends, I didn't have much of a life. I worked overtime every weekday and some Saturdays. JL was aware of the extra hours I put in, but, instead of easing my workload, he piled on more.

I carefully monitored my expenses and saved as much as I could. By the end of my first year with the firm, I had not only replenished my savings, but also increased them.

At my annual work review, I broached the subject to JL of my becoming an attorney with the firm or leaving to continue my pursuit of that career at another company. He looked at me incredulously as if I had some nerve.

"Open your eyes! Melvin Belli and I are the top attorneys in San Francisco. Most women would give their eyeteeth to be my personal secretary."

"But I put myself through law school!"

"Look here." He grabbed the morning *Chronicle* that had been opened to a picture of him dancing with a bleached blonde and flipped to the want ads. He ran his finger down the long "Attorneys Wanted" section. "These descriptions say, *'he* must have this, *he* must have that, *he* needs experience as...*he*...*he*...*he*...*he*...*he*....' There is not one single *she* in this entire section which, by the way, is one full page of columns."

I let my breath out. "I will walk into each office and personally give them my resume."

"You did that before you got this job, and it got you nowhere!" he yelled.

"But, but, maybe...."

He shook his head and groaned. "I've got a lot to do today, and I don't have any more time for this conversation. You've proven very good, and I need you to stay here. You can't leave now. We're going to be very busy the next few months. I'm taking on five new clients, including Max Rockefeller, and I don't have time to hire and train someone new. As of right now, your salary is increased twenty percent for the next year. Find a larger office and hire yourself an assistant."

I couldn't speak. Did I hear him right?

He moved toward the door, then turned around and put on his chocolate brown gabardine overcoat. "I'm off Monday for a week of rest in Hawaii. Call me at the Royal Hawaiian if there're any problems. Get a florist to deliver an Aloha bouquet to Miss Raquel MacIntosh. Her information is on my Rolodex. Sign it 'Looking forward to our trip. Love, Jay'." With that, he wrapped a plaid scarf around his neck, raised his head high, looked down at me condescendingly, and left for lunch.

The conceited bastard! He just told me I couldn't leave. That insufferable man thought he could keep me by increasing my salary and letting me hire an assistant. The room felt hot; the scent of his cologne cloying. I glared at his empty chair.

The large increase in pay after only one year at the firm was an unexpected twist. What should I do? Even if JL was a temperamental and demanding boss, working for him did carry prestige. I was privy to the personal information of some very important people. And now, Max Rockefeller joins the list. Why would he need our law firm? What kind of a case would I be working on? Would I meet him? I remembered him emerging from the lake, his clothes clinging to him, in *Return of the Dandy.* The Hollywood dreamboat reportedly broke the heart of every woman he starred with, not to mention all his male and female viewers.

I returned to my office and sank into the chair. Perhaps I should work longer at the firm. At the new salary level, my financial position would elevate from good to excellent.

I marched out to the reception area. Maude Lind stood

in front of the ficus tree gently massaging the leaves with a feather duster. She wore white gloves and had an apron tied snugly around her waist. Beside her on the floor stood a copper watering can.

So intent was she on this important job, she jumped when I said, "Mr. Lucas would like me to move into Mr. Qualms' old office right away."

Regaining her composure, she raised her eyebrows, stood regally, took off the gloves and apron, and straightened her back. I followed her down the hall and watched as she yanked the previous occupant's nameplate off the door, leaving one nail protruding from the wood like a lone pimple on a teenager's face.

Cyrus A. Qualms, Esq., had recently been fired due to his warped personality and inability to bring in new clients. He should have been fired for his lecherous behavior. The man incessantly hugged all the women in the firm, and his underarms smelled.

The space had an extra-long table that could be used for spreading out JL's cases. Unfortunately, the room was situated on the other side of JL's office from my current room and also had a connecting door.

I tried not to smile watching her stomp back to her desk.

I crossed the hall to the kitchen and poured a cup of coffee. The cleanup list on the wall caught my attention. Today was my day to wash dishes and tidy the kitchen. I returned to my office, grabbed a king-sized permanent marker, marched back, and blacked out my name with a one-inch line.

When JL returned from lunch with the Mayor, I asked him if Marla could be my assistant and the office could hire a new girl for the typing pool. I told JL his legal documents and letters deserved the best typist in the firm. With my words stressing the importance of his work over that of everyone else's, he approved the move immediately. Naturally, the other attorneys were unhappy since I had taken their best worker.

Later that day, with my door to JL's office open a crack, I eavesdropped on Maude whining to him about the change. I wondered how she had the nerve, but I would eventually find out the reason.

The firm closed between Christmas and New Year's. Marla and I wore our Sunday best on Christmas Eve and joined other shoppers at the Emporium south of Market. Thousands of lights and ornaments sparkled on the magical City of Paris Christmas tree in the lobby. The Emporium had a spectacular winter carnival on its roof. Marla and I rode the Ferris wheel, had our picture taken with Santa Claus, and laughed at the dancing elves.

25

I didn't have anything planned for Christmas day or New Year's, except to relax and not think of JL. I intended to make a nice Christmas dinner and take long walks by the ocean. I bought three books at the Emporium that were on the *New York Times* bestseller list to keep me company: *The Sea Around Us,* by Rachel Carson; *Murder by the Book*, a Nero Wolfe mystery, by Rex Stout; and *My Cousin Rachel,* by Daphne du Maurier.

Chapter 5

We were very busy the first week back to work in January 1952. JL left for court early in the morning and called in at noon to see if anything needed his attention. There were days I didn't see him at all, but I easily followed his nighttime activities in the newspaper. He attended every meeting or party of importance in San Francisco.

I spent hours preparing papers and filing documents at the courthouse. Marla didn't need a lot of direction, and there were few errors in her typing. Also, she didn't mind running JL's personal errands and fielding phone calls from his ex-wives and current lovers.

One Monday morning in April when I arrived at the office, Max Rockefeller sat in the reception area trying to read *True, The Man's Magazine*. I said trying because our receptionist was buzzing around him like a gnat in heat. In expectation of his arrival, she must have made a special trip to one of the antique stores in the Richmond District and purchased a shiny vintage stainless steel coffee server. It sat regally atop the glass tabletop in front of him on a white lace doily alongside a matching sugar bowl and creamer. I watched as she bent forward in front of him and poured coffee into a dainty little China cup with a rose motif. She had undone the top three buttons of her blouse so that he got an eyeful. When she handed him the cup, his fingers were too big to hold the handle so he ended up cradling it in his large catcher's mitt-sized hands. His eyes scanned the room, as if he was making sure that no member of the press snapped his picture.

When I got to my desk, I thought about the movie star. He certainly was an attractive man. I knew he had never been married and professed to be a confirmed bachelor, not that women were dissuaded from trying.

It turned out that Rockefeller intended to open a clothing and sporting goods store for men in the Financial District close to our offices. It was a wonderful idea. He was the epitome of a *man's man*, like Clark Gable. He couldn't have found a better law firm to prepare the paperwork. I enjoyed the time spent making sure the correct legal documents were filed and the lease agreement for the store was in order. JL helped him hire the best public relations firm in San Francisco, and, of course, JL made sure there were pictures in every newspaper on the West Coast of him and Max shaking hands in front of the new store. I remember the list of celebrities that flew in from Southern California to attend the official opening. Marla and I tried to go to the store at lunchtime, but the crowds were overwhelming.

Sadly, Max Rockefeller died ten years later from the bite of a Mojave rattlesnake while on location in a remote section of the Arizona desert filming *Sonora Dawn*. The movie director had called emergency services immediately, but Max was dead by the time a helicopter flew in to evacuate him. He died a painful death. Our entire law firm grieved his passing.

One Monday morning, JL didn't come into the office, even though he was due in court to represent Mrs. Minerva Cox-Sherwood in an unlawful detainer action. Mrs. Cox-Sherwood owned several large downtown office and apartment buildings. Normally, he would have one of his junior attorneys handle this type of case, but, even though he complained she was ornery, he fawned over the dowager because of her wealth and position. I called him at home, and he answered, his voice groggy from sleep.

"I was up late with a client." A gentle feminine moan could be heard in the background. "Get the file. Grab a cab and pick her up. I'll meet you in court." He hung up abruptly.

When we arrived at the courthouse, I escorted Mrs.

Cox-Sherwood to a seat in the front of the room. Her case was listed first on the docket. We both watched the door nervously for JL.

He still had not appeared when the judge called the case. Mrs. Cox-Sherwood was in no position to argue her side, and, without an attorney representing her, the judge would have ruled in the defendant's favor. Seeing no alternative, I introduced myself as "Jane Kitteridge, attorney with The Lucas Law Firm, appearing for Jay Lucas," and successfully pleaded her position.

Mrs. Cox-Sherwood was pleased that she obtained a judgment against her tenant but livid that JL had never appeared. "I didn't know you were an attorney," she said to me. "I see you every time I'm at the firm, and I just assumed you were one of the girls."

Outside the courthouse, I hailed a Yellow Cab and helped Mrs. Cox-Sherwood into the back seat. Just as we started to drive away, she pointed out the window. I saw JL hurrying down the street. I knocked on the cabbie's glass partition to ask him to stop, but Mrs. Cox-Sherwood slammed her hand down on the seat and told the driver to keep on moving. "That man will find out soon enough he made a mistake. I read the paper this morning. He was out late last night romancing some bombshell from Argentina! If Jay Lucas thinks I'm not important enough to show up on time, he can find another client. My new lawyer won the case. From now on, she represents me!"

JL didn't want to lose Mrs. Cox-Sherwood's lucrative account so he agreed I could handle her work, but he made sure I understood his name as the attorney of record would appear on the top line of all court filings.

It would have been nice if he had acknowledged that if I had not stepped in he would have lost her case and her account.

I felt myself smiling more, standing taller, and walking with confidence. No matter what JL said, I was definitely Mrs. Cox-Sherwood's attorney. Handling her work became my first priority. With a few clients like her, I could start my own business.

During the last few months of 1952, several highly visible trials were lined up one after another. In anticipation of court appearances and media interviews, JL commanded his tailor come to our office to recheck his measurements and create custom-made shirts and suits based on the latest men's fashions from Italy.

31

One day when I walked into JL's office with an important letter for him to sign, he stood preening like a male model in front of the full-length mirror on the inside of his door. A little man with an obvious tic knelt beside him holding a measuring tape to the hem of JL's trousers. Pins stuck out of his mouth, and glasses looped around his neck. He looked me up and down, twitched, and produced some sort of grunt.

Just before quitting time, JL called me into his office. He crunched his Chesterfield in the ashtray, sprayed his mouth with Binaca, and pointed at my outfit. "You look like one of those black and white dairy cows." I could feel my face burning. "That might have been okay when you first started this job and stayed in your office, but it isn't now. You're meeting clients and filing documents at the courthouse. You *must* look like a high-class professional secretary if you're going to represent me and the most prestigious law firm in San Francisco." He leaned back in his chair and put his shoes on the desk. The soles were as shiny as the patent leather shoes themselves. "My tailor tells me you have no fashion sense so it would do me no good to suggest you dress yourself better. He told me to send you to Macy's and let their personal stylist go to work on you."

I turned around and looked at myself in JL's full-length

mirror. Over a black pencil skirt, I wore a freshly starched white cuffed-sleeve blouse with buttons up the front and a flap pocket on the breast. My feet were encased in simple black flats. I saw nothing wrong with my appearance. I had even pinned a small red plastic poinsettia corsage on my pocket for the Christmas holidays.

He smirked at my reflection in the glass. "Get your coat. The manager of the women's department is waiting for you. You can thank me later."

I clenched my jaw and stared at him. There was no way I would pay for a new set of clothes that he wanted me to wear.

He seemed to sense my thoughts and frowned.

"I'm paying for your makeover. I consider it a cost of doing business, and I will deduct the expense. My clients expect me to have a competent secretary, one who dresses fashionably. You look like a waitress in a common diner." He slammed a file down on his desk. "Consider it your Christmas bonus."

I couldn't get out of his room fast enough. If working my butt off and tolerating his bad moods weren't enough, now the obnoxious man wanted to dress me. When I entered my office, Marla stood by my desk with a letter in her hand. I slammed the dictation pad down and took several deep breaths.

Her eyes widened when I told her what had happened.

"What are you going to do, Jane?" she gasped.

"I have a good mind to walk right out this door and not come back," I huffed.

"But, you can't do that!"

I plopped down on my chair. My stomach had started to hurt.

"Mr. Lucas has a big ego, and he's very competitive," Marla whispered. "He wants his business associates to think he's got the best secretary and that includes your looking better than anyone else's. Of course, you can't afford to dress the way he wants you to. He knows that." She picked up my letter opener and examined it. "I suppose you don't have to agree, but just think of the nice clothes you could get and how much it would cost Mr. Lucas."

Suddenly I didn't feel so badly.

I trudged to the store in Union Square and squeezed myself into the elevator filled with Christmas shoppers. A well-dressed older woman met me on the second floor. She escorted me to a small square fitting room with mirrors on all sides. I stared back at my four angry faces. She smiled and said, "Mr. Lucas told me he wants his secretary to project an impressive image to his clients; therefore, I will show you clothes that will look good on you. They will also be comfortable." She sighed. "You are so fortunate to work for such an important executive. I wish I had a working wardrobe paid for by a generous employer." She must think I've been sleeping with him.

A short time later the woman returned pushing a garment rack. "These are quality clothes from top designers that, with minor adjustments, can be worn year after year. Yes," she said looking at my eyes that had widened threefold, "Coco Chanel and Hattie Carnegie. Many of our clients are women in important positions who wear these designers. I will pair these outfits with hats, gloves, handbags, shoes, and even nylons and costume jewelry."

I looked at the tags and quickly calculated the cost. When the woman held up a Coco Chanel black quilted handbag, I salivated.

"Are you sure Jay Lucas approved this?" I stammered.

"Mr. Lucas told me it is imperative that his clients respect you, not only for your skills but for your appearance. He asked me to choose clothes that are stylish, and classic for the workplace. You should wear very few accessories to keep your look simple. Should you go out at night," she eyed me as if that was impossible, "add colorful costume jewelry."

I chose two boxy suits, one little black dress, a couple of blouses and skirts, and a warm winter coat, along with accessories. I watched the woman press the buttons on the cash register for each item, and my eyes popped when she rang up the final total. Did I buy too much? Apparently not, because she said she would charge these items to JL's account and told me to come back in early April for the new spring fashions.

After arrangements were made to deliver the purchases to my apartment building, she walked me to the beauty salon for a facial, makeup lesson, manicure, and haircut.

About 6 p.m., I walked out into the colorful glow of the giant Christmas tree in Union Square. Excited shoppers with their arms full of presents rushed around me. I touched my face. It felt soft and clean from the facial, and pleasantly cool in the night air. The sweet smell of flowers from the products used on my hair caressed my nose.

I found a space on a bench and sat down to think. What happened to my resolve to quit the firm, and how do I leave when I just accepted what amounts to a bribe to stay on? Last year Lucas dangled a higher salary and a personal assistant under my nose like a carrot, and I caved in; and now, after my second year, I'm sitting outside Macy's with a new wardrobe. Had I sold my soul to the devil?

Admittedly, I was lucky to find this well-paying job as JL's secretary. Two years ago, I had pounded the streets with a new law degree and could find nothing. What if the same thing happened again? My job with the firm would not be available to fall back on.

I stood up, buttoned my coat, and tossed the scarf around my neck. I couldn't leave the firm without having a job to go to. The only solution was to continue working for JL while I checked the employment ads and looked for opportunities.

My bouffant hairdo bobbed up and down as I headed over to Pacific Street. I hadn't intended to work very late, but the afternoon's adventure had been unexpected. JL had a court appearance first thing in the morning, and I needed to prepare notes for him.

It didn't take long to walk the short distance. A large fir wreath circled with red ribbons hung on the front door of our building. In the lobby, a white Christmas tree with red and green ornaments reached the ceiling. Underneath, nutcracker soldiers stood at attention, their rifles pointed at the front door. Poinsettia and berry wreaths hung on the walls of our office. A giant stuffed Santa in the corner smiled and waved. Someone had thrown a garland around the photograph of JL and the

President and stuck a red Rudolph nose in the middle of Truman's face. I wondered how long the picture would stay up since Ike had been elected President in November.

My shoes sunk into the carpet as I made my way down the hall to my room. I was about to turn the light on when I heard a muffled sound coming from JL's office. I tiptoed over to the connecting door and nudged it open. Moonlight from the windows spread across his Persian rug, highlighting white panties about two yards away from where I stood. Clothes had been tossed in a heap on the floor. A woman lay on her back on JL's desk emitting puppy squeals; a man over her growled. The light from the moon captured her long nails digging into his bare shoulders. I closed my eyes at the sight, and, when I reopened them, I saw black and white heels just inside the door. They were the same shoes I admired on the receptionist that morning.

I backed away from the door on tiptoes, but my purse bumped the ceramic pencil mug sitting on the edge of the desk. It smashed, and the contents rolled loudly over the blotter and onto the floor. I bolted out of my office, crunching pencil pieces into the carpet, and raced out the front door. A bus started to move from the corner stop. I banged on its side. The driver stopped and opened the folding door. I hurried to a seat, then leaned over, pretending I had dropped something so no one could see me from the street, just in case JL had managed to throw on his clothes and race after me.

When we had driven a block, I sat up and looked around. My heart palpitated, and I could hardly breathe. I stood and walked to the front. "But you just got on," the driver said, looking at me with a frown. He halted the bus. I stepped down and walked two blocks to my regular stop, looking over my shoulder the whole way.

Images of the two played over and over in my head. How long had they been having an affair? They must have heard the noise I made. Is it possible they thought the cleaners had been there, or the security guards checking out a noise?

When I got home, the packages from Macy's were sitting outside my apartment door. The manager had thoughtfully carried them up the stairs for me. I heated some soup but wasn't really hungry. I just wanted to get in bed. I tossed and turned all night until sleep eventually claimed me.

The manager turned the boiler on early the next morning, and I woke at 5 a.m. to the sound of knocking in the pipes. It would take hours for the radiators to warm my apartment. My head felt like an ice pack, and I crawled down further in the bed. Sometime during the night, Pearl had crawled under the covers, and she provided the only warmth.

Disgust with the previous night's scene hadn't dissipated. Now I knew why JL listened to the receptionist's whining about me and the other employees. I wondered how much the firm paid her.

I wanted to call in sick and stay home, but, since I'd never taken a day off, it would be obvious that I had seen them. I needed to go to work and pretend I went straight home after Macy's. Let the cleaners get the blame. I threw off the covers, put on my slippers, grabbed my bathrobe, and walked into the kitchen. I turned the stove burners on and hovered over them until the area warmed enough to make a large mug of coffee, bacon and eggs, and an English muffin. Today I needed a solid meal in my stomach.

I chose a new black dress belted at the waist. In front of the mirror, I reviewed my lesson from the day before. A quick brush of my styled hair, a little mascara, penciled eyebrows, some face powder, and I was ready to go. I put on my new black wool swing coat, walked outside, and caught the bus. I was too early to sit with Marla, but I could imagine the look on her face when I told her what I saw last night.

At 7 a.m., I arrived at the office. Pieces of the ceramic

mug were wrapped in paper towels and placed on the floor beside my wastebasket with a note from the cleaners saying they were not responsible for the breakage. My pens and pencils lay encircled in a rubber band.

I opened the door to JL's room. His Persian rug had been vacuumed, and the mahogany desk, site of last night's assignation, polished to a gleam. I could only imagine the looks of disgust on the workers' faces if they had known what they were cleaning.

It took me exactly one hour to review the files and type the material. Just as I placed the papers on JL's desk, I heard him walking down the hallway whistling Nat King Cole's latest hit, *Mona Lisa*. He appeared in the doorway and casually looked me up and down.

"Good," he said matter-of-factly. "You'll never be a beauty, but at least you now look like you can represent me and my firm." He picked up the court file, glanced at my notes, put everything in his briefcase, and left. Not a word said about last night. Did he even care that someone had seen him?

Marla told me later that one of the girls from the typing pool had to work up front because the receptionist called in sick.

Chapter 6

Marla invited me to her home for Christmas dinner. She lived with her family on Cabrillo and 47th Street, close to the ocean. The sun shined bright that day, and I decided to walk from my apartment. The breeze carried the ocean air up the avenues, and breathing in its salty essence enlivened me. I watched children playing with their new toys on the sidewalks in front of the colorful attached houses that characterized the area.

The heavenly aroma of dinner wafted toward me as I approached my destination. Marla lived in a Spanish-Mediterranean styled wood-framed house sandwiched between two similar ones. Its red-tiled roof hung low over the light-green stucco siding. The garage stood on the street level with the living area above. A large arched window faced the street, fronted by a wrought iron balcony. In the window stood a decorated Christmas tree. Sounds of Bing Crosby singing *White Christmas* came from inside.

Marla answered the door. Her brown hair hung loosely around her shoulders, and she had a small gold trumpeting

Angel pinned to her emerald-green blouse. Her skirt, a red-flared material, had a white sewn-on felt poodle in an elf outfit.

She hung my coat on the hook by the door, and we walked down the hall toward sounds of laughter in the kitchen. Four plump women wearing festive aprons stopped cooking and turned to greet me. Marla introduced her mother, a full-figured dark-haired olive-skinned woman, who grabbed me and hugged tightly. She smelled of garlic, thyme, and marinara sauce. The two other women turned out to be her sisters and the third, a niece. They shooed us out of the kitchen, and we walked through the dining room. A crystal chandelier hung over a long rectangular table. Large white dishes, shiny silverware, and wineglasses sat elegantly on a red-and-green tablecloth flaked with gold. Tall red candles in silver holders stood waiting to be lit. In the living room, ribbons and torn Christmas wrapping lay next to three little girls who sat against the wall, totally absorbed in dressing dolls. Four men played cards around a table next to the large Christmas tree that stood in front of the window. Two of them turned out to be Marla's uncles, and the other two were cousins. Marla's father dozed in a large puffy chair with his feet on an ottoman. Her brother, Carl, sat in a wheelchair, watching the men play and periodically glancing at the newest *Saturday Evening Post* on his lap. Marla had told me he had been released from the hospital, and the family had remodeled the garage into a studio apartment for him so that he could come and go without having to climb the stairs. She introduced me to everyone and then pointed to the empty space on the couch next to Carl's chair and disappeared into the kitchen. He looked like Marla with his narrow face, dark hair, and large brown eyes, but there were deep shadows under his eyes, and his skin was a pale color. I sat down, and we talked briefly about the Norman Rockwell painting on the cover of the magazine: a group of colorful Christmas shoppers waited happily at a bus stop, their arms filled with presents.

When we were called to the dining room, Marla placed me next to her brother. After her father said grace, the women served a traditional Italian feast starting with meatball soup and followed by salad, halibut with vegetables, pasta with sausage, gnocchi in red sauce, cod with basil and tomatoes, roasted capon, and more. I no sooner finished my food then more appeared on my plate. I don't remember Marla's mother sitting down. She just kept dishing out food. For dessert, we devoured sweetened figs over cheesecake while sipping espresso. After dinner, we adjourned into the living room while Marla and the women put the food away and cleaned the kitchen. I offered to help, but they said no. The men resumed their game, the children amused themselves with their presents, the radio

44

station played songs from the new *Christmas with Eddy Fisher* album, and I sat next to Carl. He told me that because his military career was over, he had taken a correspondence course in bookkeeping while at the hospital and had been hired by Playland at the Beach, the large amusement park by the ocean below the Cliff House. Pointing to his legs, he said he had been lucky to find employment so close to home. He rode his wheelchair three blocks to work and back, even on rainy, windy days. Carl had a likeable personality, and his stories about the people that came to the park were entertaining.

When it got late, Marla's father insisted that he and Marla walk me home. He patted his large stomach and said exercise was important for the digestion. Bright colorful holiday lights on houses lit our way, and their pleasant banter was a wonderful way to end the evening.

The next day, Marla and I went to Playland with tickets Carl gave us. It was a warm, sunny morning, unusual for December. I wore a short-sleeve blouse over dungarees with a cardigan sweater tied around my waist. Marla had on a V-neck tennis sweater, Bermuda shorts, knee socks, and black-and-white saddle shoes. It seemed like everyone in San Francisco spent the day there. We rode the carousel, screamed in fear from the top of the Ferris wheel, played all the games, and filled our stomachs with hot dogs and cotton candy from the concession stands, all while hearing the loud cackling of six-foot-ten-inch ceramic "Laffing Sal" emanating from the fun house. I didn't want the holidays to end.

Chapter 7

On New Year's Eve, I made a roast chicken dinner and accompanied the meal with a glass of champagne. Afterwards, I sat at the kitchen table with the bottle and a yellow legal pad, intent on reviewing the last two years with JL. It was important to put together a strategy for the New Year 1953. I had been checking the employment listings and called on a few openings that might work. I never mentioned my employment with JL but presented myself as a member of the bar working in an attorney's office as a secretary/paralegal until I found the right opportunity. Obviously, the men I talked to knew they were conversing with a woman so I received several offers to interview for the same type of work I did for JL. Of course, I had no interest in continuing as a secretary. I did make one appointment to interview for a general practice attorney; but, when I arrived at my destination, it turned out to be an upstairs office in a seedy section of the Tenderloin so I turned around.

The biggest problem I faced finding a new job was the barrier placed in front of female attorneys, not only by their male counterparts, but society in general. Sadly, less than three percent of attorneys were women in the 1950s. Companies were happy to hire "girls" as clerks or secretaries, but not for higher positions. Many had written policies that women could not make as much as men and could not be upgraded to better positions if men were available to fill them. Nothing had changed since three years earlier when I had looked for work, and, at that time, I was sure with my credentials and enthusiasm, I would find a job. Now I knew better. There were plenty of positions available for male attorneys, but they were almost nonexistent for women. If women clients across the nation had risen up and demanded that female attorneys represent them, we would have had a better chance to break the barrier. I wasn't alone in my quest. Sandra Day O'Connor, who graduated in 1952 close to the top of her class at Stanford, sought employment as an attorney but was offered a position as a legal secretary. Ruth Bader Ginsburg graduated first in her class at Columbia in 1959. When she applied to a large number of firms in New York City, she received rejections from all. Both women would later become United States Supreme Court justices.

In my last review, I again suggested JL promote me from secretary to attorney. I pointed to the legal work I currently did for him, including the Cox-Sherwood account. I told him I was just as good, if not better, than any of the men in the firm. I assured him that if he did promote me, he would

48

never regret it, and I would find and train a competent secretary as my replacement.

He laughed. "You should know by now that I'm not going to have a skirted lawyer in my firm. I'd be laughed out of town. But," he paused dramatically while I waited, "I will add the word 'paralegal' to your job description."

Then he stood like he did in court and outlined all the reasons I should be grateful to be his secretary, administrative aide, personal assistant, and, now, paralegal: he was the most important attorney in the Bay Area, his clients were the elite, his cases were high profile, he had an excellent reputation, etc., etc., etc. In other words, I was fortunate to be part of his kingdom.

He added that he was not displeased with my work and thus, after only two years working for him, my salary was high for a secretary in the Bay Area. He pointed out that he gave me bonuses and even paid my medical and dental. Finally, he held my eyes as if he was summing up to members of the jury and said I should thank him because I now looked fashionable and attractive.

My face felt hot. I barely made it back to my room before the tears began to fall. What a bastard! I had steamed at my desk all that afternoon. Just remembering that episode made me angry.

I got up and petted the cat on the chair by the window. She stretched and purred, then returned to sleep.

The office dynamics had changed since I started at the firm. In the beginning, JL had worked long hours. He had been anal in his attentiveness to every detail crossing his desk. I remember being impressed when I first started my job at how well he focused on writing letters and legal documents. He spent lots of time studying the law books in his library. He carefully reviewed his attorneys' time sheets and made sure clients were billed for every little item; however, over the months, he had gradually allocated more and more responsibility to me. I now drafted most of his correspondence and legal documents. I kept his schedule so he just needed to check in with me every morning. I prepared everything he asked and took the initiative to see what else needed to be done. Every afternoon, I talked with the attorneys in the office to see where they were on their cases. When JL arrived at work the next morning, a memo sat on his desk outlining everything in the office he needed to know. I talked directly with his clients and assured them JL would tackle their problems right away; then I set about solving them. He could make court appearances and argue cases, meet new contacts, have lunch with his friends, etc., all while trusting that, in his absence, his office ran smoothly.

Obviously, I had worked out well for JL, and he knew it would be difficult to replace me; hence, the salary increases. My pay was very good, and I received medical and dental benefits.

I also got perks on my job, like the seasonal wardrobes from Macy's and the gifts JL's clients sent him that he didn't want. On the bus home at night, I read his newspaper and magazines.

I went back to the table and poured another glass. Not only had things changed in the office, but I had changed too, the result of having a larger paycheck and an office helper. I now had more time and money to go to the movies, eat lunch or dinner out at a nice restaurant, visit museums, and take weekend day trips to Napa, Sonoma, Half Moon Bay, and Santa Cruz. Marla and I had started going to the *hungry i* in North Beach on Saturday nights to listen to Stan Wilson and the other folksingers. I loved San Francisco and the surrounding area. There were tons of things to do, and I now had enough money to do them. If I quit the firm, that would change.

So many of the women I knew hated their work but I

enjoyed my days. My hours were filled with challenging legal cases, and I could accomplish a lot because Marla had turned out to be an excellent assistant.

Still, I had planned to be an attorney and that's what I would be, even if it took a few more years. I wanted to be in front of a jury arguing a case, not sitting in the back of the courtroom watching JL emote. I wanted clients to thank me, not JL. My career had been derailed out of necessity, but I had to believe that an opportunity would present itself. Look at what happened with Mrs. Cox-Sherwood.

It had been over two years since I passed the bar, and I was still looking to practice law. I understood the reasons I stayed with the firm. I didn't want to quit, look for a job, not find one, and be poor again. I decided I was willing to work another year or two with him until I found the right opportunity; but, right now, I felt stagnant. I needed something in my life to make me feel better, a challenge, or a distraction to look forward to.

I considered my options. There weren't many that would align with my goal, except to go back to school and continue studying law. I had always enjoyed and excelled in classroom situations. If I earned an advanced degree, I would make myself more valuable to our firm and more marketable to prospective employers. The schoolwork would be interesting and test my abilities. I also might find a job through the contacts I made. At the very least, I would improve my knowledge of law.

Excited about the possibility, I filled up the first page of the yellow pad with steps to take, the first being to submit an application for a Master of Laws to my alma mater as soon as possible. Classes would start in a few weeks. I would also carefully present my case to JL because there was a chance he would pay for my education.

I flipped the page over to the next and wrote, "Finances," at the top. My account balances were very good, but the interest earned paled in comparison to the rate of return JL received on the blue chip stocks he owned. I had reviewed his monthly brokerage statements at work. He paid his broker a hefty commission for stock recommendations.

It would be smart for me to start investing in the market. Although I needed to understand buying and selling more, with the information from JL's brokerage statements I was privy to, I could start to invest fairly soon. Maybe I couldn't buy a thousand shares like my boss, but I most certainly could buy one hundred shares at a time, and I wouldn't need to pay the commission, just the trade fee. When he purchased a stock, I could too; when he sold a stock, I could sell that same stock. He would never know.

I stood up, walked over to the couch, and picked up Pearl and hugged her. She struggled out of my arms, jumped onto the chair by the window, and looked out into the darkness. Her yellow eyes followed something in a tree.

It would be nice to have a change of scenery. This studio had served me well, but I tired of the dull, furnished space. A larger apartment in a more attractive area close to the Golden Gate Bridge would be nice. I would make sure it had a large closet.

Chapter 8

On Monday, January 5th, 1953, our first day back after the holidays, I walked into the firm. Maude had already changed the pictures on the wall in the reception area. She had taken down Truman, Robinson, and Warren and replaced them with a smiling JL shaking hands with newly elected President Eisenhower and Vice President Nixon, and another of him with our new governor, Goodwin Knight. In celebration of the incoming administration, Maude had her hair fashioned short with curled bangs on her forehead like Mamie Eisenhower.

I cornered JL when he arrived and outlined the benefits to him and the firm if I returned to school. I assured him I would not take time off work to do homework or study for tests. He stared at me. After a long pause, he agreed to pay for my studies. I started school that month with classes scheduled three nights a week.

I rented a one bedroom flat on Bay Street in the Marina neighborhood close to the water. I fell in love with the Spanish-Mediterranean charm of the bright yellow house. Red bougainvillea climbed the front walls. Black wrought iron gates on both sides opened to narrow sidewalks that led to the back yard where flowers graced the perimeter of the green lawn.

I had my own separate entrance just inside the gate. My new home had previously been two large storage rooms behind the garage, but the landlady remodeled the area into a living room/kitchen, bedroom, and bath. With paint, attractive vinyl floors in the kitchen and bathroom, and wall-to-wall shag carpeting, it became an attractive space. The bedroom had a large walk-in closet, and sliding glass doors in the living room opened to the back yard. I had access to a two-car garage (even though I didn't have a car) with storage shelves and a washer/dryer.

When I opened my windows, the curtains fluttered as the ocean breezes drifted into my flat. At night, the sound of the foghorns lulled me asleep. The house had been built in 1929. Marshes and tidal pools in the Bay had been filled in for the 1915 Panama Pacific Exposition, celebrating the opening of the Panama Canal connecting the Atlantic and Pacific Oceans. Ships could transport goods from the East Coast to the West Coast without having to travel around South America. The Exposition also showcased San Francisco and the impressive rebuilding that took place in the few years following the 1906 Earthquake. During the ten months the fair was open, over eighteen million people visited the ten beautiful palaces surrounded by lush gardens that sat on over six hundred acres between the Presidio and Fort Mason.

After the Fair, the buildings had been demolished and the area developed. Only the Palace of Fine Arts, a Greco-Roman style rotunda with colonnades, remained. It was a block away from where I lived.

My landlady, Mrs. Bianchi, a woman in her eighties, had purchased the home in 1929 with her late husband. They had attended the Exposition, and she remembered walking through the beautiful gardens that her house now sat on. She regaled me with descriptions of the opulence. The Bianchi family had one son, Phil, who played for the old San Francisco Seals during the 1930s. Three of his teammates were Vince, Joe, and Dom DiMaggio. Their framed autographed pictures hung on her kitchen wall.

Like so many women of that time, she had never worked for a paycheck. Her husband handled all the family's finances. When he died the previous year, she had been shocked to find that he had mortgaged their home to pay off accumulated debt. Her attorney suggested she sell the house. Her son, who lived on the East Coast with his family, encouraged her to move close to him, but she loved the City and didn't want to leave. To earn income, Mrs. Bianchi remodeled the area off the garage. Her newspaper ad appeared in the *San Francisco Chronicle* on Thursday, January 1st, the day after I had decided to look for a new apartment.

I rented the flat the day I viewed it; then went home, packed, and moved immediately.

In the morning, the sun shone through my kitchen window. I could brew a cup of coffee and carry it outside to the backyard. Pearl would follow. Since Mrs. Bianchi loved to garden, I would often meet her there on her knees weeding. I really liked her, especially after she planted a bed of catnip.

I had never owned a TV set, but I treated myself to a 1951, 17-inch GE black-and-white tabletop with a mahogany veneer. It came with rabbit ears that I adjusted for better reception. Even so, when a plane flew overhead, the screen became fuzzy. The first night I set it up, Monday, January 19, 1953, I watched the episode of *I Love Lucy* where Lucy gives birth to Little Ricky.

I rode the bus from the corner stop to work and had a five minute walk from my flat to the law school. I easily strolled to Chestnut Street, where there were coffee shops, grocery stores, restaurants, and boutiques. I spent hours walking the area. It was refreshing to feel the bay breeze in my face while I strolled to the Palace of Fine Arts, the St. Francis Yacht Harbor, and along the shore to the Golden Gate Bridge or to Fisherman's Wharf.

Sometimes Marla would spend the weekend with me. Saturday night we could take the bus downtown, eat dinner, and see a movie or go to the *hungry i* or the *Purple Onion* nightclub. I remember in May we saw the horror film, *The House of Wax,* one of the first 3-D movies, starring Vincent Price. Everyone in the theater had to wear special 3-D glasses. That movie was so frightening, Marla and I held hands and screamed during parts. Afterwards, we were too scared to take the bus home and called a taxi. Other times, we walked up to Chestnut Street, ate, came home, and watched *The Jackie Gleason Show* and a late night movie. Sunday we might sleep in or take the bus to Sausalito or Tiburon and have lunch and shop. We loved to walk to the Golden Gate Bridge, cross to the middle, and shiver in the wind while looking down at the boats passing underneath.

JL had welcomed more clients after the first of the year, and he and his assistant attorneys spent hours at the courthouse. I carefully monitored his complicated trial schedule and made sure he left the office prepared. I returned home at night, grabbed dinner, and rushed out to school.

The trial of Senator Howard Roach went on for three months. Dubbed "Cocky" Roach by members of the press because his chestnut brown Prince Lancelot wig made him look as if a giant cockroach rested on his head, he was accused of taking bribes in return for voting favors. "Cocky" had been ensconced in congress for over thirty years and had a large following because, with the exception of this setback, he had done a lot of positive things for the community. JL paraded mothers, babies, and sick constituents through the court. They bathed the jury with tales of Cocky's goodness. The court clerk would tell me later that JL's oration was worthy of an academy award.

Chapter 9

On a warm summer morning in June 1953, Susannah De Luigi came to our office. I remember specifically it was Tuesday the 2nd because that was the day Elizabeth was crowned Queen of England and pictures of the coronation were all over the news. Laughter from the reception area reached the innards of the firm, disturbing my research on SEC filings. I put down the large tome I was studying and stood. The tittering got louder as I approached the front.

Seated on the tufted leather couch giggling with the receptionist was an extraordinarily attractive woman in her thirties. Flaming red hair offset a carefully made-up face centered by a slightly turned-up nose. A huge diamond wedding ring overwhelmed her small hand. Her fingernails were polished to match her bright red lips. A satin foulard, wrapped delicately around her neck, plunged into the bodice of the emerald-green fitted jacket that matched her eyes. Large breasts threatened to burst the buttons. Extending past the coffee table were long shapely legs ending in red high-heeled shoes with diamond straps. She looked at me and smiled.

The door to the attorneys' offices opened, and Jay

Lucas, in a gray herringbone suit and vest, smelling as if he had just emerged from a male cologne contest, strode into the room, assessed his new client, and took her hand. Their eyes locked. Pheromones expressed. I felt like a voyeur. Her knees opened slightly as she raised herself from the plush couch, an opportunity that JL's eyes did not miss. He gallantly escorted her toward his office, ogling her swaying backside in the full mid-calf emerald skirt.

After they left, I picked up the magazine she had brought with her from the table. She had been reading an article in *Vogue* about haute couture houses in Paris. A quote by Christian Dior concerning his latest collection was underlined: "I created flower women with gentle shoulders and generous bosoms, with tiny waists like stems and skirts belling out like petals." Susannah De Luigi could have been a top model for *Vogue*.

I returned to the library, but couldn't concentrate. I walked to my office, carefully edged the door to JL's room open, then sat at my desk looking through the morning's mail, one ear tilted toward their voices.

"I have recently moved west from my apartment overlooking Central Park in New York City," she cooed from the next room. "The climate is better for my sick husband,

Giancarlo De Luigi. I'm sure you've heard of him and his fleet of oil tankers."

I couldn't hear JL's response.

"It's my husband's awful family in Rome," she emoted. "They want to annul my marriage to Giancarlo. I just don't know what to do and need your help so very badly."

I suspect that she then took out a scented flowered handkerchief and brought it to her eyes.

Deciding that continued eavesdropping was beneath me, I closed the door and went back to the library. SEC filings were more interesting than JL's next conquest.

In a short while, he buzzed me.

"Cancel my reservations with…with…I forget her name. Call DiMaggio's and reserve a table for two. Mrs. De Luigi and I are walking over now."

I called the "BM" on his calendar, Miss Bettina Mulberry, and informed her that, regrettably, JL was unable to meet her for lunch. She hung up on me. Miss Bettina Mulberry was simply the flavor of the month. Even though he was now on his fifth wife, an actress from Argentina whom he met in Las Vegas, the sacred bonds of matrimony could not keep his fly zipped.

JL returned late in the afternoon. I heard him whistling

down the corridor. He approached my desk and dumped Susannah De Luigi's paperwork in the center. That night, when I had finished my day's work and placed it on his desk, the picture of wife number five was in his wastebasket.

Susannah De Luigi originally came from North Carolina, the heiress to a tobacco fortune long gone. Giancarlo De Luigi was her second husband. She had met him at a party in Rome. He was a rich Italian shipping tycoon in his late sixties with oil tankers all over the world, large yachts, and estates in Italy and Greece. When he met Susannah, he had been widowed for three months and had four children over the age of thirty who were actively involved in his business empire. Susannah had no children from her previous marriage. He and Susannah traveled to New York City where they married within weeks. His elderly Catholic parents and his children were incensed. Unfortunately, Giancarlo De Luigi sank into the depths of Alzheimer's shortly after his marriage (his family said shortly before). The De Luigi family accused Susannah of being a gold digger who took advantage of a sick man. Her response was to move her husband to California, further away from Italy. She said it was for his health. She purchased, with his money, a mansion on Belvedere Island in San Francisco Bay where he was cared for round-the-clock.

JL believed Giancarlo's family could successfully argue in court that Susannah knew her husband's mental facilities were impaired when she married him. They were prepared to bring in Italian physicians to testify. JL countered by telling them he would spend years dragging the De Luigi name and family reputation through the legal system. As a result, they proposed a settlement. We had to hire legal firms in Italy and Greece to make sure the documents read correctly in several languages and that all laws were followed. In the end, Jay Lucas successfully and brilliantly negotiated a multi-million dollar settlement for his client that included the large estate in Belvedere overlooking the Bay and a steady flow of cash. In addition, all Giancarlo's medical bills would be paid for, and, should he predecease his wife, she would receive an additional million dollars.

I did considerable research, prepared all documents, and coordinated the complex international litigation, even though I continued to study for my degree. The settlement was completed seven months later, in December 1953. As a direct result of my work, JL presented me with a $1,000 bonus.

At my third year-end review, JL raised my wages. I had decided not to broach the subject of my leaving the firm. It could wait. I was exhausted from juggling my work with the firm and going to school at night. The office would be closed the last two weeks of December, and I would be in between semesters. I just wanted to get my energy back.

Chapter 10

On a rainy afternoon in February, JL came into the office late, coughing and blowing his nose. He canceled his evening plans with Susannah. I heard the familiar *clink* of his Waterford crystal decanter contacting with the outer edge of the brandy snifter. The door to my office jerked open. He stomped in and dropped a large box of papers on my desk. My stomach turned when my nose was hit with the combined smell of Vicks VapoRub, Bay Rum aftershave, coffee, and brandy. Trapped, I backed my chair to the wall.

"I don't have time to handle all the horse manure people put on my desk and the crap I get in the mail at home," he shouted hoarsely. He blew the entire contents of his nose into a Kleenex and tossed the soggy remains at my wastebasket, missing by a foot. "From now on that's your job. Just figure out what's going on and handle it. I pay you more than enough to do that. I'm going home." He closed his red eyes and sneezed multiple times, not even bothering to cover his nose with a tissue from the box by my typewriter or the expensive monogrammed silk handkerchief sticking out of his breast pocket. He opened the door and left while I watched tiny wet particles spread across my papers.

At first I was annoyed. I had enough to do handling his legal cases, paying his bills, and solving his problems. Still, the man was my boss so I needed to make it work. I could allocate some tasks and take on more challenging responsibilities. Marla could do additional administrative work, and we would start using the typing pool. I sifted through the mess. There were invitations to social events, letters from friends, requests for donations, lots of ads, and other junk. Buried at the bottom was the first issue of *Playboy Magazine* opened to the nude centerfold of Marilyn Monroe. JL must have been really sick to forget that. He would probably come looking for it, but too late because I dumped it in my wastebasket for the cleaners to enjoy. Just the previous week, Marla and I had watched her in *Gentlemen Prefer Blonds* at the movie theater on Chestnut Street. There were handwritten notes from other attorneys in the office asking his legal opinion on a case, or if they should take on a certain new client. The men wanted to hire a couple of new typists. I laughed when I saw one attorney complain that the receptionist was too condescending.

JL's desire to control everything in the office might have worked when he first put out his shingle, but not now that the firm had grown. I asked Marla to type up a memo telling all employees that I, and not JL, would now be signing their paychecks. It also informed the attorneys that they were to submit their timesheets directly to me along with a weekly summary of each of their active cases. While she typed it up, I tromped to the front. The receptionist abruptly closed her top drawer, trapping part of what looked like a bodice-ripping paperback outside. "From now on," I told her, "continue to put all of JL's mail in my inbox but forward his calls directly to me, even when he's in the office. If anyone in the firm has any questions for JL, send them to me. Also, Marla is typing a memo to the effect that I will now be reviewing the timesheets and signing all paychecks, including yours." She started to protest, but I turned my back and walked away. If she didn't like it, she could stay after hours and discuss the matter privately with JL. This was one night I didn't intend to return to the office and interrupt the two of them.

I walked into JL's room and helped myself to a bottle of wine from the large cache he had in his closet. He would never miss the bottle, and I deserved it.

The next afternoon JL came into my office after court all sweaty and sneezing. His voice was so wheezy I thought of Andy Devine, the chubby actor who played Cookie in the popular Roy Rogers' movies. He rifled through my inbox to check his mail. After opening a few letters, he threw them back in the pile and left.

JL didn't know it, but I had just become a major player in the Lucas Law Firm. Everything of importance that occurred in our office would now come across my desk.

In September, JL flew to Washington, D.C., with his client, Clarence Littlejohn, and, of course, Susannah. He said she had friends in the area to visit but, of course, I reviewed the bills and there were two occupants in his Mayflower Hotel suite. Since Littlejohn had his own room, I could easily guess who shared JL's bed.

Littlejohn had been called to testify in front of the House Un-American Activities Committee. He had written the screenplay for the successful movie, *Gray Huskies Prowl the Congo.* He was one of many in Hollywood accused of treason without proof during the McCarthy era. A cowardly anonymous source claimed he had communist affiliations. If he didn't testify with his denial, there was a strong possibility he would be blacklisted and not find work again, like the actor John Garfield.

JL was gone for a week. When he came back, he was

pleasantly surprised to find that I had delegated all the new legal work that had come across his desk to whichever attorney I felt could best handle the case. He had no complaints.

I didn't have a lot of time to look for another job. In addition to my regular duties, I had settled into my new responsibilities and, basically, managed the office. Going to school full time proved exhausting, so I changed my student status to part time, taking only two courses a semester. That meant my degree would take four years.

I also dragged my heels on finding another position because my current salary and benefit package were higher than some attorneys in the City, and JL would no longer pay for my schooling if I left the firm.

But something more caused me to hesitate. I had been with the Lucas Law Firm close to four years, and, in that time, I had become an important part of the company. Everyone (except Maude) respected me. Whereas JL's lawyers used to go straight to JL with their questions, they now came to me, an arrangement that JL liked because it took work off his back. In turn, the attorneys were happy they didn't have to deal with an unpredictable boss.

My stock portfolio performed well (thanks to JL's

broker and a stock market that kept rising), and I continued to build up my bank accounts. I loved my flat and looked forward to going home at night. Before I studied or walked to school, I would take my shoes off and lie on the couch with a glass of wine and a snack, or one of the easy new Swanson TV dinners.

I treasured weekends with my best friend, Marla. We were both happy that the Korean War had come to a close. Over thirty-three thousand American servicemen had died in the war. Carl had lost several friends.

Before the year closed, I made the decision to remain with the Lucas Law Firm for the remaining years it would take to get my advanced law degree. I didn't have time to look for and start a new job. JL might be a pain, but I liked the work and benefits. At the end of that time, I would definitely quit. Given the anti-woman attorney bias in the workforce, I would have to start my own business, but I planned to concentrate on building a female clientele, hopefully starting with Mrs. Cox-Sherwood.

Chapter 11

In the next few years, the postwar economy continued to be robust. Business boomed, and new construction topped the charts. Large-scale vaccinations of children commenced with the Salk polio vaccine, and the first organ transplants were taking place in Boston and Paris. The Supreme Court ruled in the landmark case, Brown vs. the Board of Education, that segregation in public schools was unconstitutional.

At work, all anyone could talk about was the relationship between Jay Lucas and Susannah De Luigi. New to San Francisco and wanting to become part of the social scene, Susannah volunteered to host several prestigious charitable events at her magnificent estate overlooking the Bay. She had the gift for organization and flair so her gatherings were successful. Her husband, Giancarlo, would appear at the parties dressed in a tuxedo. He would kiss his wife, wave to everyone, and then a caretaker, giving the appearance of a friend, escorted him back to his suite. Susannah's stunning looks and perfect figure caught the eyes of San Francisco designers who gifted her with beautiful clothes in return for the mention of their names when she wore them. The beautiful red-haired Susannah became a public favorite. She appeared with JL at one social event after another, the society queen escorted by her attorney.

Susannah also shared JL's love of wine. She stood by his side at the tasting parties he hosted in Napa.

Susannah was now the "SDL" that appeared on his calendar regularly for lunch. She would come to our office, and, if he was in a meeting, chat with me until he was free. I put aside my work to talk with her. She was interesting and witty, and I enjoyed her company. She had a way of making me feel that I was the most important person in the room.

I remember January 14, 1954. JL arrived at the office dressed like he had a royal appearance before the Queen. He told me he had an important appointment at 1:00 and to make sure he left on time. After he said it for the third time, I asked where he was going. He motioned me over to his desk and whispered that the rumors in the papers were true. Joe DiMaggio and Marilyn Monroe were getting married in Judge Peters' office at City Hall, and he, Jay Lucas, had an invitation. He had been sworn to secrecy, but I later eavesdropped on him phoning his favorite reporter and bargaining the tip of the century in return for his photo appearing in the paper. Sure enough, Marilyn and Joltin' Joe tied the knot. The front-page picture in the next day's paper showed the happy couple just married. Behind them on the stairs stood a group, including the judge who married them. Jay Lucas stood beside him grinning like the Cheshire cat.

Marla, Carl, and their parents had become like family to me. They had me over for dinner regularly. I thought of her as the sister I never had. I could tell her anything, even share my deepest feelings. I found myself thinking of Carl often.

Marla worried about her mother and father. They were getting older and working long hours at the delicatessen. Both Marla and her brother were contributing to the family expenses from their paychecks. Marla's brother had started to go to their deli after work to help with the cash register and balance their books. Marla worked some nights and weekends at the store, mostly doing inventory and stocking the shelves. The good news was that the parents had plenty of food from the delicatessen to eat and had no mortgage on their house.

Chapter 12

Unexpectedly, Mrs. Bianchi passed away in March 1955, just a few days short of her ninetieth birthday. Her son and his family came from the East Coast to arrange her funeral and settle her estate. I took a rare morning off work to attend the service. I had liked Mrs. Bianchi. She was a kind woman, and she had often invited me upstairs to dinner. Sometimes I would come home late from work and there would be a note on my door telling me to check the extra refrigerator in the garage. Invariably, there would be something delicious in there to eat. That night, I knocked on the door of the main house and spoke to her son. He was a tall man in his fifties with the physique of a baseball player, which he had been. He told me he intended to fix the house up, paint, and list it for sale. He said he was sorry, but I would have to move.

I walked down to my apartment and opened a bottle of wine. I loved my flat. I loved the area. I didn't want to move. I opened the newspaper to the rental ads. There were a couple of vacancies in the area but in large apartment buildings. All said no pets allowed.

I turned the page and found five houses in the Marina for sale ranging in price from $10,000 to $12,000. The balance in my savings had been $13,000, but the bonus from the De Luigi settlement increased it to $14,000. I was saving this cash to start my new business.

Impulsively, I returned upstairs with the paper and showed him the comparable homes. I offered him $12,000 in cash with escrow to close as soon as possible. I told him he would never get a better offer. I would buy the house "as is." He wouldn't have to spend money to clear out the furnishings, fix it up, put it on the market, wait for an offer, pay a realtor's commission, etc. He could return to the East Coast with whatever of his mother's things he wanted, and I would dispose of the rest.

Bianchi was stunned by my offer. He had expected to stay in the area at least a month to wind up his mother's estate and put the house on the market. He had an appointment pending with his mother's attorney the next day to discuss her estate and get a recommendation for a realtor. I told him his lawyer could confirm the sales prices of houses in the area, prepare the paperwork, and open escrow.

I returned downstairs to my apartment and saw the wine bottle on my kitchen table. With shaky hands, I poured myself a glass. What had I done? I had never made such a large expenditure in my life, and I was only thirty-three years old.

I could barely get through work the next day. Would he accept my offer? Maybe he would try to negotiate a higher price.

When I got home at 7 p.m., there was a note on my door. I quickly went into the bathroom and splashed cold water on my face, then walked upstairs. I could hear the television blaring from inside the house. My heart was pounding. Mrs. Bianchi's son opened the door and stuck out his hand.

"We've got a deal," he said. "How soon can we get it done?"

We closed escrow in ten days. After fees and prorations, I paid $12,500 for the house on Bay Street. I now had $1,500 remaining in savings, and my stock portfolio looked good, more than enough for any emergencies, but not enough to quit my job. I would have to start rebuilding my account balances again.

The Bianchi's were very happy and left town immediately. An estate appraiser valued the furniture and paintings and sold them at auction for the family. The remaining items in the house were left for me. Although the expensive items were gone, I still had the refrigerator, pots and pans, and enough furniture to get by.

I spoke with the gardener, and he continued his service. For a small amount more per month, he would make sure there would always be flowers in bloom.

I moved upstairs into the main house and slept in the large master bedroom. On weekends when Marla didn't have to help her parents at the delicatessen, she stayed in the second bedroom, and the third bedroom became my office and study room. A large kitchen opened to a deck overlooking the back yard. On warm days, Pearl hung out there in the sun warming her old bones.

Two female students at San Francisco State rented my downstairs flat. Both had part-time night jobs on Chestnut Street. I charged them a fair amount, and the income covered all expenses for the house.

Chapter 13

JL continued to increase my salary at regular intervals and the value of the stocks in my portfolio rose. I made sure to visit Macy's seasonally for clothes and charged everything to JL.

Lucas seemed to have acquired boundless energy. Our client list continued to grow. He hired three more attorneys, bringing us up to ten, and our office space increased when he purchased the Pacific Street building and remodeled the top floor. He now had a huge office with a view. I occupied the room next to him, and Marla had an adjoining room to mine. Since we needed additional help, I had hired a clerk/typist specifically for us.

JL continued to follow his alma mater's team, the USF Dons. Led by Bill Russell and K. C. Jones, they won the National Basketball Championships in 1955 and 1956. He was a big contributor to the team, and he and his three buddies attended all the victory parties.

JL and Susannah were seen at every important event in San Francisco. She introduced him to the arts, and they attended the opera and the symphony regularly. His ego immediately recognized the advantages to being on both boards of directors, and he pushed for the positions. Our newest clients were artists, musicians, and nonprofit corporations.

It did not come as a surprise when I heard that JL and Susannah planned to purchase a winery together. They both enjoyed the Napa countryside and were a regular couple at dinners and wine tastings. They were always looking for rare wines to enjoy and had an ongoing contest between themselves to see who could find the rarest bottle of wine. It seemed like money was no barrier in their competition to outdo each other.

They found a small winery for sale in the foothills of Napa County. There were several offers for the choice property, but they outbid the others by paying an exorbitant amount, higher than the asking price. Susannah told me later that they made the decision to buy that vineyard even if it cost a million dollars.

The location was picturesque. An old farmhouse stood guarding the wine caverns and miles of staked cabernet grapes. JL and Susannah purchased the equipment and retained all employees, including the directors for operations, sales, and public relations. I was surprised at the extent of the business. It might have been a small winery, but it was first class.

Susannah and JL incorporated the business under the name Lucas De Luigi Vineyards, and escrow closed in March 1956. Both shared title equally, but she contributed the entire down payment and guaranteed the mortgage and the salaries for all personnel until the business started making a profit. JL had half the title but no financial responsibility. I knew JL was a shrewd manipulator, but how could Susannah have agreed to take on the debt for the entire business?

Susannah asked me to help organize their inaugural wine tasting party. We planned the attendance list, the tour, the tasting, the catering, the parking, the workers, and everything involved in the gala event. She had the farmhouse painted, cleaned thoroughly, and engulfed in light. The salespeople, winemakers, vineyard manager, tasting room manager and staff would be present at the gala.

It was the talk of Northern California and the event of the season. Everyone wanted to be there. Susannah had made numerous friends since she moved to California, and JL had a huge list of business associates. I fielded calls at work from people who begged for invitations. I wished I could have given one to Marla, but she seemed happy enough hearing about the preparations.

It was a warm summer evening in Napa when the guests arrived in formal attire. The governor, the mayor, and the entire board of supervisors attended. Max Rockefeller arrived in a long black limousine, and, on his arm was the Italian bombshell, Gina Del Giudice, the costar of his latest movie, *Prince Gregor Saves the Ladies of Europe*.

JL looked regal in a white double-breasted dinner jacket with padded shoulders and two horizontally spaced buttons. He preened all night and acted as if he had arranged everything. The society columnist of the *San Francisco Chronicle* devoted his entire column the next day to the fabulous party introducing the new Lucas De Luigi Vineyards.

Besides paying handsomely for my time, Susannah gifted me with an invitation to the event as a guest, several cases of wine from their new wine cellars that had been relabeled with the Lucas De Luigi name, and a blank check to purchase an evening outfit from the Dior Spring Summer 1956 Fashion Collection. When I attended the party, I too looked like one of Dior's "flower women," although I added a couple of falsies and spent the entire evening holding in my stomach.

I grew close to Susannah while working with her on the party. We had fun, joked a lot, and hit it off well. She told me she was impressed with my work ethic, and couldn't believe I was actually going to school at night. I am ashamed to say that I had originally thought of her as a gold digger, probably because I listened too much to the rumors about how she had met and married her wealthy oil tycoon husband. I now believed her when she told me she had loved him at the time. Sadly, she was caught in a quandary. Her husband dwelled in the depths of dementia, and her feelings for him had changed to a kind of devoted responsibility. Then Jay Lucas came into the picture, and she found herself in love again.

Susannah stopped by the office on a regular basis to go out to lunch with Jay. One day when he was tied up in an unexpected meeting, she asked me to join her at DiMaggio's. She looked refreshing in her blue-belted long-sleeved polka dot dress. Her red hair was pulled back into a French twist with diamond hair clips from Tiffany. Heads turned when the maître d' escorted us to JL's regular table.

"It's Jay's birthday this week, and I've planned a small intimate dinner on Saturday night for just the two of us. We've been together over three years."

I knew it was JL's birthday and had directed Marla to buy a cake for him and arrange a small office party. Everyone chipped in, most reluctantly, when the receptionist insisted we had to buy him a present.

The waiter came and bowed, offering us complimentary glasses of Chardonnay. After he took our orders, she pulled out her cigarette case and lit a Lucky Strike, winking at me. "These are the secret to my staying thin."

She blew the smoke high in the air. "I have the perfect gift for him, a 1961 rare bottle of Bollinger R.D. Champagne. I was able to get a three-liter bottle straight from France's Champagne region for only $2,700." I almost choked at the price. She took a sip of Chardonnay. "It's a fine white sparkling wine and will go perfectly with the dinner I have planned. I bet you didn't know this is James Bond's favorite champagne. Jay will love it!"

It was hard not to like Susannah. She cared about everyone and had an enthusiasm that was contagious. What I couldn't understand was her relationship to Jay Lucas. What could she possibly see in the man? I didn't have to ask. Over her glass of wine, she told me.

"I so love him." She gushed. "He's the most wonderful and exciting man I've ever met. We can't get married, at least not yet. Giancarlo is deteriorating every day, so it won't be long. I care deeply for my husband, and I'll be there for him until he dies." She inhaled smoke deeply and let it fly out her nostrils. "But Jay is my soul mate. We are destined to be together forever. When Giancarlo passes away, I will marry him. He's already asked me. I'm so happy. We've already changed our wills in expectation of that event."

The hairs on the back of my neck started to bristle. JL's will and trust were kept in our office safe, and I was not aware of any recent changes. He didn't leave anything to his ex-wives or Susannah. If he should die, his entire estate was bequeathed to San Francisco State where several buildings and a large sports center would be built and named in his honor. I wished I could tell her that, but I couldn't divulge JL's private information. Besides, I could be wrong. Perhaps he updated his paperwork somewhere other than at our law firm, although that was unlikely. I believed he lied when he said his will had been changed in her favor. It would be just like him to suggest if she really loved him she would do the same.

I watched her ask the waiter for another glass of Chardonnay.

Chapter 14

San Francisco had a new mayor in 1956, George Christopher, the last Republican to hold that office. A Greek American, he was the sole support of his family at age fourteen. He attended night school at Golden Gate, obtained an accounting degree, and later bought a small dairy on Fillmore Street. JL started hanging around City Hall and buddying up to the politicians. When the Republicans held their National Convention at the Cow Palace, JL had finagled the plum role of being part of the group that escorted President Eisenhower and Mamie to the event. Needless to say, his ego could barely fit in his head. He started talking about running for office. Fortunately, that never happened.

Marla and I didn't care too much about politics, but we were ecstatic and glued to the television when Grace Kelly married Prince Rainier of Monaco in April. If only we could become princesses. We also fell in love with the rockabilly sounds of Elvis Presley. One of my fondest memories was dancing with Marla on their living room floor. Carl cheered us from his wheelchair and joined in the singing. We couldn't stop humming *Heartbreak Hotel* and *Love me Tender*.

In late November 1956, Mrs. Cox-Sherwood walked into my office with her younger brother, Harold. He became my second client, adding several downtown commercial buildings to our account. Mrs. Cox-Sherwood hinted that if I left the firm, she would see that I had their business. I was now bringing more client money into the firm than a couple of the other attorneys. Unfortunately, I couldn't put the sign "attorney-at-law" on my desk, at least not yet; however, I was finally in the position to make a strong case to JL. I owned my house free and clear and rent from my tenants covered its expenses; my bank balance was higher than it had been before I purchased the house; and my stocks were through the roof. If JL refused to make me an attorney, I would leave the firm and open my own office. I intended to continue going to school at nights. Taking two courses a semester was manageable.

The next morning, JL arrived at the office late. His face looked bloated, his eyes puffy, a sure sign I should have waited until my review a month away; but I was too excited to keep quiet. I explained that Mrs. Cox-Sherwood's brother had asked me to represent him. "I am now doing the work for two clients in this firm. It's time for you to recognize me as an attorney. If you don't, I'm leaving."

He stood up as if he had just discovered a tack under his

bottom and stared at me. "Sit down!"

The venom in his voice, along with a massive dose of bad breath, assailed me. I wanted to ram Binaca peppermint spray down his mouth before he opened it again. Even his cologne reeked.

"I have told you over and over that a woman attorney in the Lucas Law Firm is out of the question. Forget it." He stared at me angrily. "I know what you're up to. You think if you leave you can start your own firm with old biddies like Cox-Sherwood and her brother." He put his head back and laughed.

"Yes, I think I can."

"I have taken care of you for six years. You have a superior salary and a staff under you. Do you really think I'm going to let you go? How could you even think you could steal the Cox-Sherwood accounts from me?"

Minute drops of his spit landed on my face and Hattie Carnegie dress. His hands were shaking and his eyes stared hatefully at me. I was shocked at how quickly his anger flared up.

"I have no qualms about using my power to destroy you. If you leave my employment, I'll drive you through the mud. Say goodbye to that nice house you purchased in the Marina with the money you made from my law firm."

"You have no right to treat me this way." My voice rose.

"Don't be naive. Who do you think you are talking to? I'm Jay Lucas. No other attorney in San Francisco is my equal. I'll tell everyone you're a crook, stole from my firm, and more. Who do you think they will believe?"

"That would be a lie! I've given six years of my life to this firm. You couldn't find a better worker. Look what I've done for you."

"You've seen me in court. When I'm finished with you, no one, not even the Cox-Sherwoods, will want you around." He turned and picked up the decanter on his credenza and poured himself a glass of brandy. "Go back to your room and leave me alone."

I was furious. If Jay Lucas lied and said I was a thief, I would need to hire an attorney that could beat him in court. I didn't dare argue my case alone. The fees would deplete my assets, and which of the attorneys in San Francisco would want the job? I would probably lose my house in the battle and be back on the streets. I fumed at my desk for the next couple of hours, refusing to answer the phone. Marla came into my office but retreated when she sensed my mood.

That day he left the office late, whistling Johnny Ray's "Cry me a River." I'm the one who should have been singing

90

that song. I walked to the window and watched him stride down the street as if he didn't have a care in the world. Angry, I walked to my door and opened it. No sounds in the hallway. Hopefully, everyone had gone home. I tiptoed to the office kitchen and took a Dixie cup from the dispenser next to the water cooler, then proceeded to the bathroom where I locked the door. It didn't take long to fill the cup. Then I returned to my office and entered his room through our adjoining door, moving stealthily to his desk where I sat down. His chair was still disgustingly warm. Swiveling around to face the credenza, I considered what I was about to do. It was grounds for instant termination. I removed the glass stopper from his brandy decanter and poured in the contents of the cup. The liquid blended nicely into a rich golden brown. I envisioned JL filling a snifter glass, sitting back with his feet on the desk, and enjoying the buzz.

Over the course of the week, the contents of the decanter disappeared. Every time I heard the clink of the glass, I felt better.

The holidays passed quietly. The winter cold brought concerns about the new Asian flu epidemic that was first reported in China in February. I didn't care about the flu or anything else and buried myself in work and school. It seemed like my desire to become a working attorney was a pipe dream. It would never happen. At Marla's insistence that I get some exercise, we took long walks around San Francisco on the weekends. She had even bought one of those new flying discs from Wham-O called a Frisbee, and we tossed it back and forth on Marina Green. Also, we both brought sneakers and walked the lunch hour. Sometimes we would stop at City Lights Books on Columbus Avenue in North Beach; other times, we sat on a bench in front of Saints Peter and Paul Church and watched the beatniks in their black turtleneck sweaters, berets, and horn-rimmed glasses play bongo drums and recite poetry. The smell of marijuana permeated the air. A couple of times, Marla and I must have inhaled too much because we arrived back at the office giggling.

It was a good thing I had the sneakers with me on Friday, March 22, 1957, because we experienced an earthquake around noontime. I was sitting at my desk reviewing notes from JL's meeting with Nick Harwood, the major league player who JL had first represented in 1949. He had gotten into a fight with an Irish bartender at Fisherman's Wharf because he believed there was no whiskey in his Irish coffee. He ended up destroying the bar, and JL had to bail him out of jail. As I read the police report, the room started to sway. Then I felt a rolling jolt. I grabbed my purse and tried to leave my office, but it was as if my legs didn't work. Everything shook, and I heard screaming. Realizing I couldn't get very far, I crawled under my desk, wishing I was anyplace but the top floor of a brick building. It seemed like a long time before the motion stopped, but, in reality, it was less than a minute. I quickly put the files away, locked my desk and filing cabinet and headed toward the stairs along with everyone else. JL ran in front. The street was filled with people escaping from the buildings, some hysterical. Later I heard one person had died and there were several injuries. The magnitude of the earthquake was 5.7, causing damage primarily in the Daly City area, but also stopping the Ferry Building clock. No one wanted to go back to our office because of the aftershocks. Since I had locked my desk, I decided to go home. The buses weren't running, but I put my sneakers on and walked.

Sadly, when I got home, I found Pearl lying dead on my bed. She was nineteen years old and had been with me since she was a kitten. I could not find any sign of what had happened. It simply looked like she had died of old age. When I finally stopped sobbing, I wrapped her in my bed sheet and carried her to the back yard. I buried her among the catnip plants and placed a small stone as a marker.

In December, after years of night classes, I successfully completed my final exams, and the school awarded me the Master of Laws Degree with a specialization in taxation. JL took on more tax cases and assigned them to me. Of course, he took the credit for my work.

I checked the newspaper every day and watched the postings at the State and local government offices. There still weren't many positions a woman could fill. JL had me boxed in anyway. Even if I found something, without a work references for the last seven years, no one would hire me.

I rewarded myself with a driver's education course followed by the purchase of a new Volkswagen beetle convertible in the horizon-blue color. My first drive in my new car was up and down Lombard Street, known as *the crookedest street in the West.* Weekends, Marla and I would travel the coast of California with the top down, weather permitting. Occasionally, Carl came with us. Marla and I helped him into the front passenger seat, and his wheelchair fit in the back. We often stopped at the Lucas De Luigi Vineyards for lunch. JL and his friends were usually there in the bar. If Susannah was present, she always greeted us warmly and treated us to glasses of wine. Time seemed to fly by.

In early 1958, Susannah called me at lunchtime. She was in a telephone booth outside the Tadich Grill. JL had not shown up for their luncheon date. When our receptionist told her he wasn't in, she asked to speak to me. Did I know where she could reach him?

"Hold on," I told her. "He's in his office."

I knocked on his door and opened it. "Susannah's on the phone."

He didn't look up. "Tell her I'm not here."

"But I already told her you were."

He glared at me, and then picked up the phone. I closed the door.

I knew JL had revved up his pecker again. Just last week, the gossip columns hinted that a well-known attorney was frequenting the Tiki Lounge at Trader Vic's and having mai tais with an unnamed exotic brunette. Also, he and his buddies flew to Las Vegas for a long weekend. He told me he had an important interview with a prospective client, but I knew better. He was also coming in late to the office, finding fault with everyone and leaving early. One night when I worked late as I often did, JL was still in his office. About 6 p.m. he came out and told me to go home. I cleared my desk, grabbed my purse, and left. Maude Lind was still at her desk in the reception area. She was holding a mirror and fluffing her hair. I could smell Chanel No. 5. I stared at her when I went by, but she quickly averted her eyes.

A couple of months later, Susannah and I went out to lunch. She looked tired and drawn and picked at her salad.

"Jane, I don't know what to do," she said. "He tells me he loves me and takes me to fabulous events. Our photographs are always in the newspaper. But a lot of times he ignores me." Her eyes filled with tears. "He's also running up huge bills at the winery. He uses a fancy limousine service to ferry guests back and forth to Napa, and, unbelievably, he had a swimming pool built in July. I didn't find out about any of these expenditures until the bookkeeper called asking me to add $20,000 to the winery account."

"How did he explain that?"

"He said we needed a limousine to pick up our clients. But, Jane, they are really his friends, especially those three idiots who hang around him. Well, he calls them his business associates, but you and I both know they're his bar buddies. He built the pool next to the farmhouse because he said we could have wine tasting on the deck." She examined her bright red fingernails. "He sends cases of wine to clients and friends." I knew JL had a closet full of Lucas De Luigi wines at the office and handed them out to clients. I helped myself to a couple of them a week.

Since I knew that no checks were being issued from JL's bank accounts to the winery, Susannah continued to foot the bills. It seemed like he enjoyed spending her money.

She stared at her glass of wine. "I want to marry Jay, but the doctor now says that Giancarlo may linger on for some time." She put her glass down and looked at me. "I know that Jay has been seeing other women." She searched my eyes, hoping for me to say something positive.

I sipped my Chardonnay and waited.

"He may have these occasional flings, but he'll always love me."

She took another bite of salad. "Everything is stressful. I can't eat or sleep, my stomach hurts, and I just don't feel well."

Lucas became even more obnoxious. He growled at the other attorneys. In spite of his rude behavior, they stayed with the firm. Did he threaten to withhold his references and accuse them of theft too? He had also started to pad his time sheets and overcharge our clients. A couple of them had called questioning their bills. The few times I brought the subject up to JL, he said he had worked at home. Since I could see no additional notes in the files, I had my doubts. Why would he do that? Our firm made plenty of money. I thought about the winery. He owned half, but Susannah paid for everything? He owned our office building, his personal residence, and he had no debt. It didn't make sense. Unless he just did it for the sake of doing it.

Chapter 15

In the weeks after our luncheon, I called Susannah several times. Her maid always told me she was busy. Finally, in September, she phoned, apologized for not getting in touch, and invited me to her home Sunday afternoon.

It was a lovely drive across the Golden Gate Bridge, up Highway 1 onto Tiburon Road, and along the shore to Belvedere Island. The sun was bright and sailboats dotted the Bay. Susannah and Giancarlo lived in a beautiful two-story mansion surrounded by large elms. The grounds were a mass of flowers. As I pulled into their circular driveway, I saw Giancarlo being wheeled around by a man in uniform. The caretaker was carrying on an animated conversation, but Giancarlo stared straight ahead without responding.

A maid answered the door and escorted me through rooms filled with plush furniture and expensive paintings to the family room, where large windows showcased sparkling ripples on the water. Susannah sat on a lounge chair, her legs wrapped in a colorful blanket. Her face was heavily made up, but even that couldn't disguise the sunken cheeks and glazed eyes. On her head was a red wig teased into a pageboy. What had happened to her? She threw the blanket aside and struggled to her feet, her body frail in a simple white blouse, loose black Capri pants, and ballet slippers.

She hugged me. There was a smell to her I couldn't quite identify, but it wasn't perfume.

"What's happened to you?"

"I'm sick," she said.

"What's wrong?"

Tears rolled down her cheeks. She reached into the pocket of her pants and brought out a tissue and wiped them away. "I should have answered your calls, but I always expected to get better. Come outside with me and I'll tell you everything. I've had chairs set up near the water."

We walked out the sliding glass door and down the path toward the dock. Susannah leaned heavily against me. Two brown rattan chairs with cream cushions had been set up around a table with a large sun umbrella overhead. The view toward San Francisco was spectacular. As soon as we sat down, a maid appeared with crackers and cheese. Susannah asked her to bring a couple of glasses of Chardonnay and some sandwiches.

"The last time we met, I hadn't felt well. I thought it was

100

the stress with Jay, but I finally went to the doctor."

"Susannah, I should have called you more often. I would have come and helped."

"The doctor said I could have an operation for the cancer, but it will just buy me nine more months of painful days."

We were silent, staring at the sailboats as they raced across the open water.

The maid came back with a large tray and placed it on the table. Susannah picked up the plate of sandwiches and offered me one.

"I've missed our conversations," she said.

I watched helplessly as she took a deep breath.

"I've come to accept that Jay cheats on me. It's as if he can't help it." She took a sip of Chardonnay. "I also know he's been awful to you. He couldn't keep his law office going any more without you doing his work and making sure everyone else did theirs. And he knows it. He'd be laughed out of town if his clients found out you did everything. Jay Lucas is not the wonder boy he used to be."

I doubted she knew the extent of his cruelty; his threats to accuse me of theft if I left his employment.

Susannah took a cracker and nibbled. "Remember I told you he ignored me for a while. Now that he knows I'm sick, he calls me every day and comes here several times a week to profess his love for me. He says he will marry me the minute Giancarlo dies."

"Susannah," I said, trying to control my emotions. "He never told me you were sick. Why didn't he mention it? I could have been here for you."

"I should have picked up the phone and dialed your number, but I didn't want to upset you. I've been so happy for you living in the house you bought, and now you have another law degree and a nice car."

My heart felt heavy as I looked at her.

"I believed I would get better. But now the doctor says there is no hope. Sadly, I will probably not outlive Giancarlo."

I reached over and took her hand.

"Jay is only coming to see me because he knows I've willed him my share of the winery, the house, and a large amount of money. He orders my staff around like he owns the place. Yesterday, I saw him looking out at the dock in front of us smiling, dreaming. I know he was envisioning living here.

She seemed so tired, as if it was a great effort to sit with me. "A few years ago, I named him executor of my estate.

Besides the bequests I made to him, there are large sums to go to different charities, and Giancarlo is to rejoin his family in Rome where they will care for him."

Saliva dribbled from the side of her mouth. She wiped it with a napkin. "It's awful to not be in control of your bodily functions."

I looked away. Why would she leave that bastard anything?

As if reading my thoughts, she said, "Can you understand that, despite his behavior, I love him. I'll always love him, even in death. We belong together."

A seagull landed close by and stared at us.

"I've asked you here because I need your help. I want to write farewell letters to my friends and plan my final days, but I don't have the energy to do everything myself."

"Of course I'll help."

"I'll pay you handsomely."

"No, Susannah, I don't want your money. I've got plenty of vacation and sick days accrued."

"I've had a wonderful life, done things that other women only dream about. I don't want anyone to feel sorry for me. I want them to celebrate my life." She sighed. "My body will be cremated here in Marin County. You know I've always loved the water. There's a yacht at one of the piers in San Francisco. I will charter it for a luxury party. You and my friends can dine on fancy hors d'oeuvres and toast me with glasses of Lucas De Luigi wine while you spread my ashes." She started to sob.

Three months later, Susannah died.

Chapter 16

I drove to the pier and boarded *The Dearly Departed* with the other guests. When we had arrived to take Susannah on her last journey, reporters and photographers were waiting. The *San Francisco Chronicle* society columnist was there. He had written a very moving column that morning, "San Francisco's princess has passed away." JL was a study in feigned sadness. He gave several interviews, preening, as usual, and emoting that he was there to celebrate the life of a beautiful, gifted, and wonderful woman who had been his best friend and client. Reporters took notes like they were attending a coronation. Everyone knew that, if it were not for Susannah's husband's prolonged illness, she and JL would be married. It seemed a tragic love story because now that marriage would never take place.

I had wanted to look fashionable for this event so I spent a lot of money on a special Dior frock I knew she would have loved, a sleeveless red bodice above a skirt of green petals. Over my arm, I carried a fitted jacket to match the skirt. My dress represented a perfect tulip. With the jacket on, it became a bud with the hint of the flower underneath. On the seat beside me lay Dior's red wool coat I brought to put on if the weather became chilly, and, on my feet, Dior's floral sandals. Red plastic-rimmed cat eyes sunglasses with sparkles on the upper right completed my outfit.

Shortly before she died, Susannah had gifted me with a large diamond stickpin in the shape of a branch covered with ruby berries. I had pinned it carefully over my breast and the jewels sparkled in the sun.

For the next couple of hours, we cruised around the Bay. I mingled with Susannah's friends and listened as they spoke fondly of her zest for life, her love of the arts, her pet charities, and more. JL stayed in the cabin, standing at the bar surrounded by his cronies. They hung on his every word. JL's continued bragging about his successful legal cases nauseated me, more so than the pitch and roll of the yacht, so I moved to the deck for fresh air and sat by myself at a small table.

I enjoyed the warmth of the sun on my clothes, the cool breeze on my face, the salty smell of San Francisco Bay, and a glass of bubbly champagne. Sounds of laughter surrounded me as Susannah's guests ate, drank, and reveled.

A crewmember set a plate of filet mignon, bacon-wrapped shrimp, cheese tarts, and marinated white asparagus on the table. I ate heartily and wished Susannah sat next to me. Actually, she did. I had placed the container with her ashes in a beautiful blue Tiffany bag on the deck by my chair.

With dusk approaching, we neared the Golden Gate Bridge. The time had come. The boat slowed and rocked gently. JL stepped up onto the long bench that extended the length of the back of the yacht. Everyone gathered to watch the ceremony.

He turned to us, his face a mask of sincerity. "It is with a heavy heart that we must say goodbye to our precious Susannah." He put his hand on his chest and looked down.

"And now," he said, "final words from Susannah herself."

I handed him the letter she had written. He opened it and, shielding the paper from the breeze, read loudly so all could hear.

"My dear friends. Do not grieve for me. I have led a wonderful life. This cruise is my last gift to you. Enjoy yourselves, and think of me with fondness."

Tears came to my eyes when I remembered her struggle to write the words with her shaky hand.

"And to my darling Jay."

He touched his heart and looked to the sky as if she benevolently smiled down at him.

"I wanted to leave you something special."

I watched him pause in expectation and to draw the moment out.

"Do you remember four years ago when we first started our contest? We vied to see who could find the rarest bottle of wine, and we continued our game for special times. Well, my love, last month I successfully bid at Christies for a bottle of Jeroboam Chateau Mouton-Rothschild 1945. I paid over $100,000."

Jay's mouth dropped open, revealing white sharks' teeth. He grabbed the rail to steady himself. It took minutes for him to regain his composure.

"We will share this bottle together, just you and me. You may drink as much as you wish, but no one else may have any, not even a sip. It is our last communion together. I wish to leave you with the pleasant taste of the finest wine you have ever had, the nectar of the gods. When you have finished and are sated, the remainder is mine. Pour it with my ashes into the Bay. I will love you forever. Susannah."

JL sent up a large roar to the heavens and shouted, "What a gift!" He stepped down from the bench. I reached into my briefcase for the wooden wine box that contained the prized bottle. I had brought a flat screwdriver with me and inserted it into a small opening, prying the lid open to reveal its contents.

JL grabbed the bottle from the straw that sheltered it, his hands shaking. "I can't believe this cost over $100,000!"

He returned to his platform, standing tall and regal, his floral Waikiki shirt flapping in the breeze. "I wish I could share this with all of you, but only Susannah and I will enjoy this exquisite wine." He looked down at everyone and laughed. "You can only dream." Sounds of disappointment filled the air.

His face lit up. "Someone take a picture! Who has a camera? I want to preserve this moment for eternity." He held the bottle close to his face and proceeded to pose in various positions. His friends laughed and accommodated his request.

Convinced that enough pictures of him had been taken, JL jumped down from the platform and studied the bottle, giving the impression that he could actually read the French words. After demanding a corkscrew from the waiter, he seized it and shoed the server away, then ripped the seal himself and twisted the cork out. A wine glass magically appeared. He poured in a small amount and swirled it around, assessing the color. Closing his eyes, he brought the glass to his nose, took a deep smell, and groaned in pleasure.

The group was quiet in anticipation. JL lifted his glass and looked directly at the Tiffany bag I was holding.

"To Susannah," he proclaimed.

"To Susannah," we echoed.

He slowly sipped the wine, continuing his orgasmic groans. "Ah, it is perfection itself. Dry as sunbaked grapes, but sweet as heaven."

Several of his friends pleaded for a taste, even offering large amounts of money, but JL said no. "This is for me, and no one else, except, of course, my Susannah."

He closed his eyes again and raised his head. His lips graced the rim of the glass as the wine slowly ran into his mouth. His body moved in tandem with the gentle thrust of the boat.

"My God, I can't believe Susannah spent over $100,000. It's worth every penny."

He called to a crewmember. "Bring more drinks and hors d'oeuvres for everyone."

He took the Tiffany bag from me and held it high in one hand, his glass of the treasured wine in the other.

"Susannah, I can't top this! You've won the final contest."

JL handed the bag back to me, then poured himself more wine.

Crewmembers came and refilled our glasses, and we toasted Susannah again, and again, until the Captain came and told JL to spread the ashes soon because the weather was turning. JL gave him a dismissive nod of the head. He had no intention of speeding up his minutes in the spotlight. But the captain was right. The wind had started to pick up. It blew my hair into my face. I took my glasses off, reached for my coat, and put it over my shoulders. I could see dark clouds closing in, and the sailboats on the bay were racing home. The smell of rain was in the air.

We spent another half hour listening to his oohs and aahs until JL finally had his fill and stifled a belch. Only a few ounces remained in the bottle. His speech had started to slur and his eyes glassed over. I could tell he didn't want to give up the bottle, but he stepped back onto the bench and faced us with the pretense of a gentleman. "It's time for Susannah to enjoy this marvelous gift with me."

He reached for the Tiffany bag and opened it. Surprised, he looked up. "There's another letter." He pulled it out.

"It says 'to be opened after my ashes have been dispersed and the remainder of wine poured with them'." JL looked like a happy birthday boy about to blow the candles out on the cake. "I feel wonderful," he shouted to no one in particular. Anxious to open the second letter, he garbled his words, "I'm going to spread her ashes."

He reached his hand into the Tiffany bag again and brought out a plastic container. As careful as he could be after having imbibed so much, he took the lid off, extended his arm over the stern, and slowly let Susannah's ashes fall. They were picked up by the wind and dispersed into the water. The boat rolled back and forth, forcing him to bend slightly and hold onto the rail for support. He poured the remaining wine into the Bay. I stepped up on the bench beside him to take the empty bottle.

A crewmember brought a bouquet of long-stemmed red roses, and JL tossed them into the water. Together, we watched as the wake dispersed Susannah's ashes, the wine, and the flowers throughout her beloved San Francisco Bay.

Small drops of rain started to fall, and the boat lurched. Concerned crewmembers hovered close by, anxious to herd us into the cabin for protection from the elements. In spite of the obvious discomfort of everyone around him, JL grabbed the second letter and opened it as if it were an announcement of an academy award.

"My dear Jay," he started, then stopped abruptly and looked up. His eyes were teary and rimmed in red to match his nose. "Sorry, everyone, I think this may be personal." He read silently, a boyish smile on his face.

In seconds, his features changed into a frown, and, then, a look of disbelief. "It can't be," I heard him whisper. His eyes widened. His face, already blushed from the wine, streaked scarlet.

"You bitch!" he yelled, fists high in the air as if Susannah dwelt in the heavens above. His face became ugly and twisted. He clutched his throat, turned his body, and thrust his arms over the side of the boat, as if trying to bring Susannah's ashes back. He screamed into the water, "You goddamned bitch!"

I stood on the bench beside him, not knowing what to do. The others rushed toward us to help. The weight of their bodies caused the stern to dip violently. Water splashed over the rail, soaking everyone and flooding the deck. Several people fell. I tumbled off the bench. The empty bottle flew out of my hands and smashed. I landed in the shards of glass. Jay Lucas thrashed on top of me.

"Get back. Get to the middle," I heard someone yell. "The boat will go over!"

JL grabbed the lapels of my coat and pulled me against him. I thought he was trying to help, but his cold hands moved up and gripped my neck. His eyes looked at me with hate. *He knew! He knew I had helped Susannah!* Strange, guttural sounds came from his throat. I grabbed his wrists, trying to wrest them from my neck. "Let me go!" We rolled together on the deck.

I tried to get to my feet and away from him, but the boat continued to seesaw. I couldn't release his grip. The sea spray blinded me, and frigid dampness embraced me with a deathly chill. I heard people screaming for lifejackets.

The boat took another violent lurch, and his hands fell away from my throat, but he grabbed my wrist. "Stop. Let me go," I sobbed. My other arm flailed in the air, desperately trying to find something to hold onto. He dragged me up on the bench toward the rail of the yacht. The boat dipped again, and he half fell over the side, keeping my wrist tight in his fist. I struggled for my life. *"Please, no, I don't want to die!"* I slammed against the rail of the boat, and felt the pain of a prick on my breast. Dear God, the Tiffany pin!

I ripped it off and stabbed his arm, over and over. Maniacal eyes glared at me, through me. He wouldn't let go. He reached under my leg and with superhuman strength hoisted me into the air. In a last-ditch effort, I desperately struck out with the pin, into his hand, his wrist, wherever I could reach; and, finally, when he brought his face next to mine, I plunged the pin into his eye. He howled and let go of me. I fell onto the wet deck. A strong blast of wind rattled the masts and the rigging. Terrified, I watched him drop backwards into the water.

Glass from the smashed bottle imbedded in my arms and legs. The salt water stung the cuts like bees pricking a powerless victim over and over. "Help me," I cried. My hands were covered in blood.

Epilogue

More than sixty years have passed since *The Dearly Departed* sailed from the pier in San Francisco with Susannah's ashes. JL's body was never recovered. His remains, if any after the sea creatures feasted, lay somewhere in the Bay or have drifted with the tide under the Golden Gate Bridge and out to sea, perhaps to find a home in the hold of one of the numerous sunken ships off the California Coast.

Without a body or evidence to prove otherwise, the police concluded that JL died accidentally. Several eyewitnesses swore under oath that he had consumed most of the bottle of the Mouton-Rothschild wine and was drunk. They saw him standing precariously on the bench at the stern as violent gusts of wind rolled the boat. They stated that he appeared unsteady from inebriation, and that he lost his balance and plummeted into the swirling water.

Surprisingly, no one saw JL try to kill me. Instead, the witnesses painted me as a heroine. To them it looked like I tried desperately to save him and almost lost my life in the process.

The public never accepted the official findings. There were too many unanswered questions. What caused the sudden change in JL's behavior just before he plunged over the side of the yacht? Why did he profess his love for Susannah while spreading her ashes in the Bay, but then, suddenly and dramatically, clutch his throat, raise his fists to the heavens, and curse her?

Without a body, medical examiners could not determine JL's condition when he plunged into the water. Was he drunk? Did he have a medical emergency? Is it possible he was murdered?

The letters that he read from Susannah were not salvageable. The wine bottle had been smashed to smithereens. His so-called friends sold the pictures they had taken on board of JL to the highest bidders.

Rumors surrounded his death. Perhaps a disgruntled person or group murdered him. For years, the press hounded an attorney who had been fired by JL and threatened retaliation, even though the man was overseas when the events took place. The romantics believed he became angry because his beloved died and left him alone. I personally prefer the speculation that Jay Lucas did not die after he plunged over the side of the yacht. It entertains me to consider the theory that he swam to shore and disappeared into anonymity. A variation of that story circulated. JL had been killed because he secretly worked as a spy for our government and he possessed knowledge harmful to the Russians. There were also those who believed he escaped over the side of the yacht into a waiting boat where special agents escorted him into a witness protection program.

Last year I saw a documentary about him on TV. It pictured JL as San Francisco's legendary litigator who had won millions of dollars in judgments during his legal career, a super star who was larger than life; a man who loved the limelight. It listed his clients as if they were royalty. Black and white newsreels showed some of his interviews following successful trials. Court strategists spoke glowingly of his deep, resonant voice, and the way he stared at each woman in the jury until her face turned crimson. A well-known law professor stated that Jay Lucas was the ambulance chaser of the legal field, quick to arrive on the doorstep of any big named individual or company with troubles on the horizon.

Viewers saw his plush penthouse on Nob Hill. They saw the auctioneer drop the hammer when his Jaguar was auctioned off. The new owner of the Lucas De Luigi vineyards in Napa, Marcus Storm, the retired race car driver, happily showed the property and regaled the TV audience with tales of the goings-on at night in the room by the underground wine cellar.

JL would have loved everything being said about him. But the portrayal of his romance with Susannah De Luigi could have been made into a best-selling movie. The documentary portrayed them as two famous charismatic lovers caught in a terrible triangle, desperately enamored with each other, but unable to wed. A helicopter flew over Susannah's Belvedere mansion. The documentary ended with newsreels of her lavish funeral at Grace Cathedral followed by the return of *The Dearly Departed* to the pier in San Francisco after the tragic loss of her lover, the famous San Francisco barrister. The narrator ended with the question, "What really happened to Jay Lucas?"

I think of Susannah often. She was a kind and gifted woman, but a weak one. I can't fathom how she could have loved Jay Lucas. What possessed her to name him the beneficiary of her large estate?

In her final week of life, he came every day and told her he loved her, while constantly glancing at his watch as if he had better things to do.

Three days before Susannah died, one of the caretakers

found JL standing, a pillow in his hands, over Giancarlo as he slept. He told the worker he was making Giancarlo more comfortable. The staff member told Susannah that if he had not stepped into the room, he believed JL would have smothered Giancarlo. Since his death was expected, there would be no questions, and JL would have gotten away with murder.

JL was not satisfied with the large inheritance Susannah had planned to leave him. The greedy rat smelled additional riches. The large settlement he had negotiated with the De Luigi family included the provision that if Giancarlo predeceased her, she would receive an additional one million dollars. Given his health, no one expected Giancarlo to outlive his wife.

JL's sense of dishonor rose to the occasion. I have no cause to doubt what the worker said. JL had come close to killing Giancarlo so that he would die before Susannah and JL would inherit the million dollars.

I had visited early that evening and sat with Susannah. She was quite lucid when I arrived, and visibly angry. She told me what JL had done.

"Giancarlo will die in his own time," she said, "but I know now Jay tried to kill him. I didn't realize the extent of his greed. He's not satisfied with everything I am leaving him. He wants more." She struggled to talk, tears cascading down her face. "I never thought he would go so far."

She begged me to stay and prepare a new will for her that night. She signed it early the next morning with the caretakers witnessing her signature. Her estate would be placed in a charitable trust, her banker the executor. Money was set aside so that Giancarlo could return to Rome and be cared for by his family.

JL stopped by the next day, but no one mentioned the changes. I advised the workers not to leave Giancarlo for a minute; then went to Susannah's bedroom where he was sitting next to the window looking bored.

When I entered, he ignored Susannah who appeared to be asleep on the bed, and asked me when I would be back to work. I told him I was still on my vacation time and Marla could handle everything.

"Marla's okay, but she's not as good as you. I want you back because we've got a large estate to probate coming up and we need to prepare." He stood, took his hat from the table, bent down and kissed the prone Susannah on the top of her head, and left.

I looked at Susannah. Her eyes opened wide. She had not been asleep.

She struggled with her words. "Did you hear that? It's my estate he's talking about." She moved her head to the side and cried. "How could I still love him so much that my heart aches?"

She looked at me. "I'm concerned for you. When he finds out you made a new will for me and he gets nothing, he will destroy you. I must do something, but I am so tired. I can't think straight. I just wish JL would die with me. Then everything would be so easy."

We looked at each other. She sunk back in the pillow and closed her eyes. I held her hand, and the truth poured out of me. I hated JL. He wouldn't let me leave the firm to become an attorney in my own right. If I tried, he would lie to everyone and call me a thief. He would take everything from me, my house, my savings, my reputation. I told Susannah how helpless I felt over the years as I watched my dreams disappear.

She sat up and slowly reached her hand to my face to gently wipe away a tear.

"I want to take him with me," she whispered. She sank back into the pillow. "I think I know a solution for both of us, but I need you. Help me into my wheelchair."

I took her into the yard. We moved down the path and looked out at the Bay. A couple of sailboats were in the frigid water, and a large container ship headed out to the ocean. She pointed out the belladonna bushes growing wild in the shade of her garage with their beautiful shiny black berries. I picked a handful and placed them in a small bag.

Returning to the house, I helped her sit at her desk. She wrote the second letter Jay read on the yacht.

"My darling Jay, by the time you read these words, your heart will be beating rapidly, your vision impaired, and your throat will be dry. I promise you the poison in the wine is quick acting and your death will be rapid. I will not leave this world without you."

The day after Susannah died, I went to her safe deposit box with my power of attorney and removed the wooden wine box that had been shipped directly from Bordeaux, France. I placed it in my briefcase and returned home.

That evening, the delicious aroma of boeuf a la Bourguignon filled my house. I had purchased the ingredients that afternoon, and the classical French dish simmered on my stove. I felt the night's activity warranted an unforgettable dinner.

With surgical gloves, I opened the wooden box. There, cushioned in straw, sat the bottle of Jeroboam Chateau

Mouton-Rothschild 1945. I carefully picked it up, steamed off the seal, and uncorked the bottle. With steady hands, I poured a glass. Then I set the table and brought out my good linens and china. While delicately sipping one of the world's most expensive wines, I slowly ate my elegant meal.

After dinner, I brought out the shiny belladonna berries that Susannah and I had gathered, and placed the ripened fruit from the deadly nightshade into my blender. The beautiful black color splashed the sides. I carefully poured the liquid through a sieve to separate the pulp until I had enough to displace the quantity I had consumed. Then I poured the juice into the bottle and watched the wine darken into a lush crimson color. The cork fit perfectly back after I gently tapped it with a hammer. Finally, I glued the seal in place and put the bottle back into the straw nest awaiting it in the packing box. I hammered the lid shut, then rinsed the blender and put it into the garbage.

I never thought myself capable of murdering anyone, but helping Susannah kill JL was the only way to free myself from the rope JL held around my neck. It would be easy. No one would suspect me of the murder. After all, I was his faithful secretary for nine years. If blame were to be given, it would go to Susannah.

I did not try to wipe away any existing fingerprints and had been careful to wear gloves. Even if JL's body tested positive for poison, it would be Susannah's fingerprints on the bottle.

I needn't have worried. Forensics played no significant part in the investigation. There was no body, the glass bottle had been smashed to smithereens on the deck, and Susannah's letters were not salvageable.

I had no reason to remain at the Lucas Law Firm. I tied up the loose ends on JL's desk and turned over his remaining cases to the other attorneys. I said goodbye to Maude and the others. After nine long years, I walked out the door.

The Cox-Sherwoods hired me to handle their legal work and manage their commercial and apartment properties. They provided me with a suite on the ground floor of one of their large buildings in the financial district. My new office had three spacious rooms with large windows looking out onto the busy sidewalk. I made sure "JANE KITTERIDGE, ESQ." appeared in large letters on the glass pane nearest the front door. I hired Marla to assist me and paid for her to go to law school. Over time, I added more attorneys to handle our increasing workload, and diversified our areas of expertise.

I had the successful career I always wanted. I became one of the most sought after lawyers in San Francisco. I am proud to say my firm welcomed female graduates from law schools. When San Francisco became the hub of the women's liberation movement in the sixties and seventies, we were at the forefront.

To this day, I still live in the same house in the Marina that I purchased from Mrs. Bianchi's son.

Marla's brother was the last tenant to occupy the flat on the ground floor. It was a sad story, and I grieve for Marla every day. She became one of the best attorneys in my new office. Sadly, absorbed in reading legal documents on her way to the courthouse, she stepped out into traffic on Van Ness Avenue and was killed instantly. Her parents never recovered from the shock. Her father had a fatal heart attack shortly after. A few months later, her brother lost his job when Playland at the Beach closed. Marla's mother was forced to close their delicatessen, sell the house, and move in with her sister. Marla's brother could have joined them, but the second floor apartment had no wheelchair accommodation.

I gladly offered my downstairs flat to Carl. There were no steps to negotiate, and he could easily wheel around the area to the shops. I hired him as my firm's bookkeeper, and he worked three days a week. He enlisted the retired Navy veteran who lived across the street to be his driver/helper. They became friends, and I could often hear them laughing in his rooms below me. Carl's mother came frequently to visit and help him with laundry. On those days, she spent hours in Carl's kitchen making meals for us.

Carl and I grew very fond of each other. I suppose you might say he became my significant other. The Marina was a wonderful place to live, and I easily walked beside his wheelchair as we wandered around the area. There were several excellent restaurants and shops a few blocks away on Chestnut Street. We looked forward to our nights together.

I try not to think of JL, but persistent members of the press continue to track me down. Of course, I have become somewhat of a minor celebrity myself, the top female attorney in San Francisco who just happened to work for Jay Lucas and was on the yacht when he died. There was also gossip that JL and I were more than boss and secretary. What a nauseous thought.

Carl is gone, Marla is gone, and I'm over ninety years old. I don't feel well, and I know my days are numbered. There is no longer the need for mystery. JL was murdered on the funeral yacht, and he deserved it.

Will I be forced to atone for my sin in the next world? I hope not, but sometimes I wake at night with a recurring dream. JL is lying on the ocean floor. He is beckoning me to go to him, entreating me to take the pin from his eyes.

About the Author

Mary Miller Chiao has won awards for historical research from the California Pioneers of Santa Clara County. *Adirondack Life Magazine* published her memoir of summers in the Adirondack Mountains in the 1950s, and an album of material from that time frame has been on display at the Kinnear Museum in Lake Luzerne, New York.

Her fiction appears in *The California Writers Club Literary Review*, *Good Old Days*, and *Carry the Light*. She has won literary competitions at the San Mateo County Fair and the National League of American Pen Women, Nob Hill, San Francisco branch.

She is a member of the National League of American Pen Women, Santa Clara County Branch, the California Writers Club, both the Peninsula and South Bay Branches, and is a contributing editor to *WritersTalk.*

Mary resides in Northern California, and *Death on the Funeral Yacht* is her first book.

Made in the USA
Monee, IL
26 October 2020

46116534R00079